She could ha

At the very leas
face away from
fraction too long
contact was soft, a gentle brushing lighter
than a moth's wing which left her light-headed
with the need for more. For long moments
they were lost in each other, then he muttered
hoarsely.

'Mmm?' Rebecca mumbled distractedly
before their mouths could fuse. 'What did you
say?'

'I said, what a waste. . .'

Instantly, Rebecca stiffened. 'A waste, is it?
So much for your apology!'

Dear Reader

In Caroline Anderson's ONCE MORE, WITH FEELING, Emily and David meet again after their divorce, in HEART ON THE LINE Jean Evans' Georgia goes to Ethiopia after a broken engagement, and in Australia Meredith Webber's Elly has A DIFFERENT DESTINY. We're very pleased to introduce new author Josie Metcalfe, whose Rebecca and Alex have NO ALTERNATIVE but to respond to each other. With such good reading, how could you not have a wonderful Christmas? Enjoy!

The Editor

!!!STOP PRESS!!! If you enjoy reading these medical books, have you ever thought of writing one? We are always looking for new writers for LOVE ON CALL, and want to hear from you. Send for the guidelines, with SAE, and start writing!

Josie Metcalfe lives in Cornwall now with her long-suffering husband, four children and two horses, but for an Army brat frequently on the move, books became the only friends who came with her wherever she went. Now that she writes them herself she is making new friends and hates saying goodbye at the end of a book—but there are always more characters in her head clamouring for attention until she can't wait to tell their stories.

NO ALTERNATIVE

BY

JOSIE METCALFE

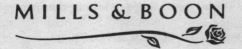

MILLS & BOON LIMITED
ETON HOUSE, 18–24 PARADISE ROAD
RICHMOND, SURREY, TW9 1SR

For BM, for believing in me,
the Mylor Mob, and Caroline.

*MILLS & BOON, the Rose Device and LOVE ON CALL
are trademarks of the publisher.*

*First published in Great Britain 1994
by Mills & Boon Limited*

© *Josie Metcalfe 1994*

*Australian copyright 1994   Philippine copyright 1994
This edition 1994*

ISBN 0 263 78885 7

*Set in 10 on 11½ pt Linotron Times
03-9412-54549*

*Typeset in Great Britain by Centracet, Cambridge
Made and printed in Great Britain*

CHAPTER ONE

REBECCA paused before she opened the door into the reception area and smoothed deceptively slender hands over the rich auburn of her hair to check its neatness, then gave a final tug at the hem of her hip-length white coat. Turning the handle, she walked through into the airy brightness of the reception area she had taken such pride in decorating.

'Mrs Marshall?' Rebecca felt again that unmistakable thrill as she met a new patient.

'Yes, dear. I'm Phyllis Marshall. Shall I come through now?' She was a small, slender woman, dressed with quiet good taste in a pale blue suit, her silvery grey curls elegantly styled.

'Just a moment, Mother.' The words were gentle but the deep voice was commanding. 'I need to ask a few questions before we go any further.'

Icy grey eyes were turned on Rebecca and the figure she had not seen sitting in the chair in the corner rose to his full height.

For a moment, all Rececca's attention was taken by the sheer presence of the immaculately grey-suited man confronting her. How could she not have seen him? He must be several inches over six feet tall and with shoulders any rugby player would be proud of. Her lightning-fast inventory included a full head of dark hair which appeared slightly ruffled, as if either the wind or his own lean-fingered hands had combed through it.

But those eyes! Those icy grey eyes. As soon as her

own gaze encountered them, she was mesmerised and a chill like the touch of a cold finger made its way up her spine and teased the hairs on the back of her neck.

'I take it you're the receptionist?' Once again the words were gentle, but this was obviously a man accustomed to being in charge of a situation, accustomed to being right. Before Rebecca could correct his misapprehension he continued.

'I cannot allow my mother to be seen by this Dr James until I know something about his qualifications. Where he trained, whether he is a member of the Association, or whatever it is—that sort of thing. Is there anyone here who can answer those sorts of questions?'

One dark eyebrow was raised, but otherwise the chiselled perfection of his darkly tanned face was quite expressionless as he waited for her answer.

Surreptitiously taking a deep breath and slowly releasing it, Rebecca hoped her voice would not betray the fact that her pulse rate was galloping.

'I am Rebecca James.' She paused briefly, sending up a prayer of thanks that she sounded so calm. 'You are quite right to make sure that practitioners are properly qualified. I attended the Anglo-European College of Chiropractic and am a Member of the British Chiropractors' Association.' She indicated with the wave of one slender hand the framed certificates she had proudly hung on the pale apple-green wall before she turned towards the diminutive figure still seated on the toning sage-green chair.

'Is there anything else you would like to know, Mrs Marshall?'

'Oh, no, my dear. Dorothy Frost told me all I needed to know. She was the one who recommended I come to you, you know. She was so pleased with what you did for her.'

'I'm glad I was able to help her. Please, give her my best wishes when you see her.'

The sound of a gentle but unmistakably masculine cough broke into the conversation.

'*You* are the chiropractor my mother has come to see? This is *your* practice?'

Remembering in time how very unprofessional it would be to comment on his rudeness, Rebecca held on to her temper with an effort and replied courteously.

'Yes, I am the chiropractor and yes, this is my practice.' She flicked a quick glance up at the clock on the wall before continuing.

'I like to see my patients at the time they have arranged and I have another new patient due in half an hour, so, if you don't mind. . .' She allowed the sentence to die as she turned to Mrs Marshall. 'If you would like to follow me, I'll take you to a cubicle so that you can get a gown on.' Turning and picking up the folder lying in readiness on the counter, she led the way across the reception area.

She was standing beside the open door when she realised that her patient was being closely followed by a large, imposing shadow.

'I'm sorry, Mrs Marshall, I didn't realise you needed help with undressing.' Rebecca's voice was sympathetic.

'Oh, no, my dear. I haven't reached that stage yet, thank God.'

'Then. . .' Rebecca turned her full gaze to the man who loomed behind 'why is. . .'

'I am coming through with my mother,' he announced firmly, his eyes as glacial as ever.

'I'm afraid that isn't your choice to make.'

'Do you mean to tell me that you are preventing me from accompanying my mother?' Although the volume was unchanged, the voice was filled with cold anger.

'Not at all.' Rebecca kept her voice stiffly polite, 'Any patient over eighteen years of age who comes to see me has the choice as to whether they come in alone or prefer their partner to come in with them. As your mother is over eighteen it is her choice whether she lets you come in the consulting-room with her—after all, it is her body!' She knew her little joke had fallen flat, but she was unprepared for the brief flash of fury she glimpsed on his face before it resumed its apparently habitual impassiveness.

'Well, Mother,' he commented blandly. 'It seems it's your decision. . .' He paused, waiting for her answer.

'Well, then, dear, if you'd like to wait for me out here, I'll go through to get ready.'

Rebecca was hard pressed not to laugh out loud at the expression of stunned incredulity which crossed his handsome face as he realised he had just been calmly dismissed.

Within half an hour Rebecca had escorted Mrs Marshall back through to the reception area.

As she opened the door, she was unwillingly aware that her pulse-rate was increasing at the prospect of a further confrontation, but the room was bare.

'Oh!' Mrs Marshall murmured as she, too, realised her son's absence. 'I wonder why he decided to wait in the car?' She gave a dismissive shake of her head before concentrating on booking her next appointment.

'I would like to see you in two days' time, Mrs Marshall. Will that cause any problems for you?'

'Not at all. If Alexander—my son—isn't able to bring me, I shall order a taxi.' She huffed out a resigned breath. 'I do hope you'll be able to help me, my dear. It's such a bind not being able to drive myself about, especially as I've only recently had the time and opportunity to learn how!'

'Well, as soon as I've developed those X-ray plates, you'll be able to see what you look like from the inside.' Rebecca hesitated for a moment before continuing. 'Some of my patients like to have their partner come in with them when they see their pictures. If they're a little nervous, it can help to have someone else there to ask questions.'

'If my son is free, may he come with me? He is bound to understand more of the technical words.' She chuckled.

Rebecca's heart sank at the memory of the man's air of disapproving animosity, but smiled her agreement.

'Of course he may, Mrs Marshall, if you would like him to,' but, *oh, please God, don't let him be free. . .* Rebecca's thoughts winged upwards in a heartfelt wish as she escorted Mrs Marshall out, marvelling at how deceptive first impressions could be. No one would ever guess at the life of grinding poverty Mrs Marshall had endured in her determination to provide for her two children after her husband's death; her cheerful serenity would seem to belong to someone who had never known trouble or want.

How could such a lovely lady have such an abrasive son?

Knowing that her next patient was due at any moment, Rebecca stayed in the reception area. Until the practice became a little busier, she had decided to save herself the expense of a receptionist, and it was not until she watched the door of a steel-grey BMW open that she realised that she had been idly following Mrs Marshall's progress across the parking area.

A dark head appeared over the top of the car, swiftly followed by a large amount of a very broad pair of shoulders. She couldn't hear what comment Mrs Marshall made, but her son laughed openly in response.

This time Rebecca's heart lodged somewhere in the base of her throat as she saw the change that laughter made. Gone was the expressionless mask which he had maintained in her presence. This face was stunning in its animation and Rebecca knew with awful certainty that this side of Alexander Marshall could be—*was*— very attractive. With her eyes glued to the smile which lingered while he spoke to his mother, Rebecca revised her estimate to *dangerously* attractive, and her pulse-rate agreed.

Unfortunately, by the time she had finished work for the day, her brain had caught up with itself and she was filled with questions.

It would have been impossible for her to have reached twenty-four without knowing that the male half of the population in general responded to her striking appearance. Her feminine pride was piqued that when she had met Alexander Marshall her slender five-foot-five frame, topped as it was by a gleaming wealth of red-setter-coloured hair, had not had any visible effect—either that, or he had superhuman control over his reflexes.

Her other major disappointment was the blow to her professional pride. It was by no means rare for people to fear the unknown, whether it was complementary therapy such as chiropractic or the more serious prospect of surgery. With Mrs Marshall's son, though, it was more a case of outright antipathy towards her profession, if not total condemnation.

This was the battle she had been waging for the last

six years, ever since she had decided to make chiropractic her career, and she would not allow anyone to
disparage either her choice of career nor how she ran
her practice. Still, she found herself dreading the
possibility that Mr Alexander Marshall would accompany his mother to her next appointment and sit there
like some stone-faced monolith.

Her thoughts had been racing around while her
hands had busied themselves with the rather mechanical chore of developing the X-ray plates she had taken
that day and reloading the cassettes with fresh films.
The expense of having her own X-ray equipment
installed in the specially prepared room had been
extremely high, but she had not been willing to offer
her future clients anything less than the best service
possible.

In Mrs Marshall's case, it meant that she would be
able to reassure her both verbally and visually that her
fall had not caused serious damage, while in the case
of her second new patient the X-rays confirmed, as she
had suspected, that the patient had quite severe degeneration of the femur head and acetabulum and was in
urgent need of replacement surgery on both hips.

As was customary in such situations, professional
ethics required that a report be sent to her GP with the
recommendation that she be referred immediately to
an orthopaedic surgeon.

Rebecca flipped through the list of specialists she
had compiled when she moved into the area and
inelegantly snorted her disbelief.

'Not *another* Marshall to deal with,' she marvelled as
she copied the name down. 'Well, I hope for the sake
of my poor patient that you're a bit more human than
the last one I met!'

* * *

'Hello, Mrs Marshall.' Rebecca's step was light as she walked into the waiting-room to find her patient entering alone. 'Was your son not able to come with you, then?' She was amazed to find that instead of the sheer relief she would have expected, she felt almost disappointed that she would not be seeing Alexander Marshall today.

'Oh, it's such a nuisance,' the older woman's voice had an exasperated tone. 'Just as I was expecting him to collect me, I had a phone call from his secretary asking me to take a taxi as he'd been unavoidably delayed.'

As Rebecca ushered her through to the changing cubicle, Phyllis Marshall continued to chatter.

'He's taken some leave to complete some research and do a series of lectures, but they still keep calling him in. I think he's working harder than ever. He hardly has any time to relax any more. . .' Her voice faded into a background noise as Rebecca's mind took off on its own track. Obviously his start in life hadn't prevented him from becoming a high-powered professional in great demand as a consultant. Well, that certainly fitted with her impression that he was accustomed to being in control. In their first encounter he had almost stunned her with the power of his personality, and although he had been disapproving of her, she found herself unaccountably looking forward to the next occasion when they would cross swords.

Rebecca had no sooner sat Mrs Marshall in a chair in the consulting-room than there was an unexpected rap of knuckles on her door.

Excusing herself to her patient, she crossed the room to open it and found herself looking up and up into an uncomfortably familiar pair of icy grey eyes.

'Mr Marshall. . .' Her voice sounded quite breathless as her heart thumped rapidly with surprise.

'Alexander, dear. You managed to get away after all.'

Rebecca took a hasty step to the side and opened the door wide enough to admit the breadth of his shoulders.

Peversely, he paused before entering. 'I *am* permitted to enter?' The voice was calmly polite but, as usual, was backed by a hint of steel.

'Certainly.' Rebecca was glad her tone exactly matched his. 'Your mother was hoping you would arrive in time.' Warily she held out her hand in greeting, fully expecting that it would display the fine tremor which had started inside her. A sharp tingle raced up her arm as the warm strength of his palm enfolded the slenderness of hers and, startled, she drew away.

'*Unlike you*?' The quietly spoken words were for Rebecca's stunned ears alone as he passed suffocatingly close on his way into the room.

So swiftly had he moved that she had no chance to retaliate privately to the barb, and the smiling look of gratitude on his mother's face made it impossible to say anything in her hearing.

Rebecca closed the door while she mentally drew her cloak of professional competence around her, then turned to smile at her patient.

'As I was saying, Mrs Marshall, there is no major problem causing your neck and shoulder pain. You haven't broken anything. . .' Rebecca paused uncertainly as a small but clearly audible sound reached her. 'Is anything the matter?' Her query was intended for her patient, but it was her son who answered.

'Are your findings borne out by the X-rays? You did tell my mother she would be seeing them today.'

'Yes, she will. I usually preface showing the pictures by a short explanation, but if you would rather——' Rebecca once again directed the question to her patient '—I can show you the pictures first and then take you through the diagnosis and my proposed treatment?'

'Oh, my dear, I don't suppose it will make much difference to me either way, but I must admit, I've been looking forward to seeing for myself what's going on in there!' Her expression was almost gleeful.

'Right, then.' Rebecca withdrew the two plates from their protective envelope and clipped them in position on the viewbox, switching on the enclosed light.

'These are the two pictures I took on your first visit. As you can see, one was taken from the side view and one face-on.'

Rebecca continued her explanation, checking at frequent intervals to ensure that Mrs Marshall was following and, when she detected any puzzlement, making sure that her words were clear enough for her obviously non-medical patient to understand.

'So,' she concluded, 'although you have evidence of wear and tear in your neck, due probably to the types of work you used to do, it wasn't really causing you much of a problem until you fell. Then, the shock to your neck was rather like a whiplash and your neck has seized up.'

'How do you propose treating my mother?' It was the first time he had spoken since she had started her explanation, but Rebecca had been aware through every pore of her skin that he was standing right behind her shoulder. Reluctantly, she turned to face him and was amazed to see that he was standing several paces away. But he had felt so close, almost as if his body was within inches of touching hers.

Hastily she looked towards a still slightly apprehensive Mrs Marshall.

'Initially, I will just use simple techniques for releasing the muscle spasm and increasing the mobility of the neck.'

'It all sounds delightfully vague and simplistic.' The deep voice seemed to become colder with each word. 'Do you actually have a recognisable medical diagnosis?' It was almost a taunt; a challenge to her to prove herself and the worth of her chosen career all over again—as if she hadn't spent the last six years doing just that.

The redhead's fabled temper, which she usually kept under strict control, slipped its leash.

'Yes, Mr Marshall, I *do* have a recognisable medical diagnosis. Your mother had a fall which, on top of years of wear and tear, has caused the muscles of the cervical region to go into protective spasm. She has suffered a degree of soft tissue trauma and, due to the radicular involvement, is also experiencing discogenic brachialgia paraesthetica. Now, are you any the wiser with all the big words?'

Rebecca stopped abruptly, appalled at the lack of professionalism in what she had just done. Her cheeks burned and her hand flew to cover her lips as if she could recall the fateful words. She was stunned to hear Mrs Marshall chuckling heartily.

'Oh, my dear, that's why I wanted him to come with me. I didn't know that you would explain everything so clearly. I thought I would need him to decipher all those incomprehensible long words you medical people seem to love.' She laughed again delightedly.

'But. . .' Rebecca was still nonplussed. 'I'm sorry, Mrs Marshall, but I still don't understand. . .'

'Oh, no, my dear. It's my fault entirely. I've just realised that. . . Oh! How stupid of me! I didn't think to tell you that Alexander has just started working at St Augustine's.' She named a well-respected London hospital and Rebecca's head turned sharply, her dark gaze clashing fiercely with icy grey eyes as his mother continued proudly. 'He's one of their top orthopaedic surgeons.'

Rebecca was horrified. Only by sheer good fortune was she not standing there with her mouth hanging open.

Everything suddenly clicked into place so that the clues all made sense. Now, she was even more appalled by her outburst. What on earth must he be thinking of her? Her brain scrabbled frantically for logical thought.

He had been antagonistic towards her from the start, but, after this. . . She pulled her mental processes to a sharp halt. Enough! This was no way to conduct herself.

'Well, then——' Rebecca forced herself to speak crisply '—Obviously you are perfectly conversant with the terminology of your mother's condition and will be able to answer any questions she may think of once she returns home.' She allowed her eyes to meet his briefly and surprised a fleeting expression which almost looked like approval at the speed of her recovery.

She forced herself to look away immediately, before he could have a chance to discover that her cool calmness was just a shaky pose.

'In the meantime, Mrs Marshall, if you would like to come over to the couch here, it's time we started doing something to make your neck and shoulders feel a little easier. After all, the sooner you're feeling better, the sooner you'll be able to drive yourself about again.'

'Oh, my dear, that will be wonderful. Alexander is so good, giving up his precious time to run about for me, not to mention taking my dog for walks, but I must admit I'm looking forward to having my independence back!'

It was amazing how blind some mothers could be to the faults of their offspring, Rebecca mused, as she made sure Mrs Marshall was comfortable.

'Do you want your son to stay in the room while I treat you, or would you prefer him to wait outside?' Rebecca heard the hiss of a sharp intake of breath, but before he could start to speak, Mrs Marshall broke in happily.

'Oh, no, dear. I'm quite happy for him to stay. You never know,' she added mischievously, 'he might even learn something!'

This time Rebecca heard his snort of disbelief quite clearly and shot him a lightning glance of reproof before she shut out all the external distractions and concentrated all her attention on treating her patient.

'Right, then. If you'll just relax and let me take the weight of your head. . . Good. Now I'm going to move it gently this way and then you'll probably hear a sharp click—a bit like someone cracking their knuckles. . . Well done! Now I'll test your range of movement again. . .'

'Oh! Well, I never did! That feels so much easier all ready. And all you did was crick it like that.' She turned her head gingerly so that she could see her son. 'Did you hear that, dear. Wasn't it extraordinary?' She obviously didn't want an answer, and she didn't get one, her son standing to one side like a silent sentinel while Rebecca completed the session.

When Mrs Marshall went out to dress, Rebecca completed her notations in her file and stood to leave the room.

A movement seen out of the corner of her eye startled her as she realised that her strong lingering awareness of the presence of Alexander Marshall had been no phantom.

'Very slick.' The softly spoken words could have sounded like a compliment if she hadn't been watching his expression. His position in the corner of the room meant that the light fell across him, outlining the almost perfect profile—only the slight bump of an old injury to the bridge of his noise spoilt the perfection—and striking a gleam off each curve of his slightly windblown dark hair.

He straightened away from the wall suddenly, the movement of his powerful body controlled and fluid, and made his way towards the door. Pausing briefly and turning at the threshold to spear her with icy grey eyes, he spoke in his usual quiet tones.

'I may not be able to accompany my mother to every visit, but you can be sure that I will be monitoring her progress—or otherwise—very closely.' And he was gone.

The phone was ringing as she entered the treatment-room the following morning, and she hurried across to answer it, spurred by the sharp twist of anticipation deep inside which whispered, 'Maybe. . .'

'Rebecca? Rebecca James?' Her heart sank as she heard the voice on the other end. Why had she expected that it would be Alexander Marshall, and why on earth should she feel disappointed that it wasn't? She perched herself on the corner of her desk and forced herself to concentrate.

'I'm sorry,' she stammered, suddenly aware that her caller was waiting for an answer. 'Yes. This is Rebecca James. Can. . .?'

'Hello, Rebecca. This is Tony. We were talking at the BCA Conference last month?'

'Oh. Yes, Tony.' A mental image of his craggily handsome, middle-aged face flashed in her memory.

'You remember we were talking about the trials being set up to evaluate the different ways of integrating chiropractic into the NHS?' He paused briefly and in the silence she heard him shuffling papers. 'Look, we've got a bit of a problem in your area. We had a scheme all set up and ready to run but Don——' he named her nearest colleague '—has had to drop out due to ill health.'

'Oh, no.' Rebecca liked her older colleague, a true gentleman of the old school. 'Nothing serious, I hope?'

'No, nothing serious,' Tony confirmed hastily. 'His wife finally made him go for his hernia repair!'

Rebecca joined in with his laughter, then took a quick breath as realisation struck her and her hopes rose sharply.

'Why did you want to speak to me?' She tried to keep the excitement out of her voice in case she was wrong, and opted for the more obvious suggestion. 'Does Don need some locum work done?' She found herself childishly crossing her fingers—as if that would make any difference—and held her breath while she waited for his reply.

'I think he's got that covered, but you could always give him a ring. No, the reason I called is to tell you that your name was suggested as Don's replacement in the trials.'

All of a sudden the air in her lungs whooshed out.

She had hoped, but never expected to have such an opportunity so soon.

'Replacement?' she echoed, the significance of the word suddenly hitting her. 'But won't Don be——?'

'You don't mind a bit of blunt speaking, do you?' Tony broke in. 'Only we've hit several snags with this one, not least the fact that Don's wife has been pushing for him to do less work, rather than more, and has persuaded him to see that his op. is the ideal time for a rethink. Someone also pointed out that your age might count against you, but as far as your knowledge and expertise goes, your academic and postgrad records speak for themselves, and if anyone still carps there are always your family connections to throw at them.' He made a silencing noise as he heard her try to break in. 'I know, that's the last thing you want to do, but——'

'No, Tony.' Her voice was determined. 'If I don't do it under my own steam, I don't do it at all. My "family connections", as you call them, have nothing to do with it.'

When he remained silent, she bit her lip at the thought that this golden chance might be slipping away, then straightened her shoulders sharply. 'I mean it, Tony. On my own merit or not at all—it would do nothing for the validity of the trials. Anyway, you don't need me to lean on my family connections. Don has already set up all the contacts, hasn't he? Where are the trials being held, and who is the specialist in charge there?'

'I'm sorry, didn't I say?' His tone was apologetic and there were further sounds of papers being sorted before he continued, wearily, 'That's the other problem we've had. There's been a major reshuffle at their end, too. They've now designated St Augustine's, which actually works out better for you as far as travelling to the initial meetings and all the updates are concerned, but the orthopod there is a new chap too. First-class reputation, but a bit of an unknown as far as his attitude towards chiropractic is concerned. His name is Marshall. Alexander Marshall.'

CHAPTER TWO

REBECCA rubbed her body dry briskly. She had over-slept this morning, but nothing and no one was going to be allowed to make her late for this morning's meeting. Alexander Marshall was not going to have any excuse to find fault with her—not if she could help it.

Luckily she had been better organised last night and had left her clothes ready. It had taken some consider-able thought, but, as she got dressed, the mirror reflected what a perfect choice she had made in the businesslike jade-green slimline suit teamed with a creamy silk blouse.

As she rapidly applied the minimum of make-up between hasty swallows of coffee, she had managed to catch up on all but five minutes of her planned time.

She was just about to switch on her telephone answering machine when the phone started to ring.

'Oh, no!' Rebecca wailed helplessly. Now she would have no option but to pick it up. Perhaps she could answer it as if she was the machine. . .? But as soon as she lifted the receiver she knew that wouldn't work.

'Rebecca?' She recognised her mother's brisk voice only too well. At least she knew that this would be a brief call; her mother was not one for chatting. 'You haven't forgotten that we're picking you up on our way to the dinner-dance this evening, have you?'

'No, Mother. I hadn't forgotten,' she lied quickly. Well, if she hadn't overslept, she'd have had time to look in her appointment book and diary and then she'd have remembered!

'Right, then. We'll be with you between six and half-past, depending on the traffic, so you will be ready and waiting, won't you? See you, then. Bye.'

'Bye.' Rebecca murmured into the broken connection again and put the receiver down. 'Botheration!' she muttered fiercely to herself as she picked up her briefcase again and pressed the button to set the answering machine. 'The *last* thing I'm going to feel like doing tonight is smiling like a good little girl, but. . .' she heaved a sigh as she locked the door and approached her car '. . .it is Father's big night, so. . .' Resignation filled her voice before she turned the key to start her journey, and she was swamped by the realisation of her destination and the fact that she was now going to be very pushed for time. So much for making a good impression.

'Ah! Dr James!' She was sure that steely voice would haunt her forever. 'We were just about to give you up for lost.' Alexander Marshall's glance flicked towards his companion seated at the table in the small conference room. 'Have you met Mrs Barker? She's in charge of the physiotherapy end of the trials. Ellen, this is Rebecca James.'

Ellen Barker nodded gravely, her faultlessly styled hair and immaculate uniform making Rebecca all too conscious that she hadn't had the time to find a mirror after her mad dash across the hospital car park and along the seemingly interminable corridors.

Of course, *he* was dressed as impeccably as ever, the sleek fit of his charcoal-grey suit sitting perfectly across the breadth of his shoulders, the pristine white of his shirt accentuating the healthy tan of his skin.

'If you'd like to sit.' It was definitely the voice of Mr Consultant-Orthopaedic-Surgeon taking charge. 'We'd better get this meeting under way. I'm sure we all have other things waiting for our attention. Now,' he started briskly, 'I presume you've had some sort of briefing from your. . .' his gaze dropped to the sheaf of papers spread on the highly polished table in front of him '. . .BCA?'

Rebecca sat, smoothing her hands down the sides of her skirt to settle in comfortably. Drawing in a surreptitious deep breath to prepare herself for what was obviously not going to be an easy meeting, she forced herself to meet his gaze squarely for the first time.

Only, he wasn't waiting for her to start speaking at all. Instead, his cool grey eyes were taking a leisurely inventory of her face and figure which, far from annoying her, caused a sharp twist of excitement deep inside her.

So! He wasn't quite as immune to her as he had tried to pretend. The unexpected pleasure which that thought gave her was the boost she needed to set her on an even keel.

'That is correct, Mr Marshall.' Her voice broke into his perusal of the modest V of cream blouse revealed by her suit, and his eyes jerked back to her face. 'The British Chiropractic Association.' And you knew that very well, after the grilling you gave me the other day, her own eyes challenged him.

'Unfortunately——' her shaky voice strengthened as she continued '—owing to various changes of location and personnel, we have each come into this with less than adequate time for preparation. So——' she smiled at each of her counterparts '—if we look on it as an ideal chance to build a really strong team right from the start, perhaps it will turn out to be a beneficial

experience?' Rebecca leant back against the comfortable upholstery of her chair conscious that, although
she had been utterly polite, she had definitely thrown
down the gauntlet.

'A team.' The steely tone matched the ice in his
gaze, telling her that the challenge had been taken up.
'You envisage this developing into a team effort?' He
glanced briefly at Ellen Barker before continuing.
'Surely it is up to you to prove to us the worth of what
you are offering?'

'Not at all.' Rebecca kept her words calm, although
she had started to seethe. 'The value of chiropractic
treatment is not on trial here. That has already been
demonstrated in the MRC trials several years ago. The
only things on trial at the moment are the best methods
of incorporating chiropractic so that it is available to
those who need it without having to go ouside the
NHS.'

'So. . .' he drew the word out slowly, holding her
attention effortlessly '. . .you are expecting to be given
carte blanche with all the patients being referred to this
department by their GPs? Do you think that was what
they intended when they made the referrals? Do you
think the patients themselves will be happy to be
shunted aside after reaching their turn on the waiting
list? I don't think so.' He shook his head, the vehemence of the action showing what his quiet tone did not.

'I think,' he continued inexorably, 'that they would
be appalled to wait for weeks, maybe months, in pain,
hoping for an early appointment with an orthopaedic
surgeon only to find when they arrive that they are
handed over to some complementary therapist!' He
made it sound like a profanity as he sat back in his
chair, apparently calm, but the hands resting on the

sheaf of papers were knotted so tightly that the bones gleamed whitely through the skin at his knuckles.

Rebecca's gaze flashed from his hands to his face and back again, for a moment unsure whether he even realised how much tension he was revealing. Suddenly he moved, and his hands disappeared from view. Rebecca glanced up quickly and was startled to glimpse the slight reddening which had appeared along the smooth perfection of his cheekbones. It would seem that the impervious monolith was developing cracks even as she watched.

'That is not my understanding of the situation at all.' Rebecca made sure that she spoke clearly. 'My briefing is that this trial will be evaluating the most efficient use of chiropractic expertise. It is not intended to be in contention with surgery or physiotherapy, but as an adjunct.'

'How, exactly, do you see this happening as far as the physiotherapy department is concerned? We certainly can't cope with any more patients than we already see. There isn't enough space and there aren't enough hours in the day!' It was the first real contribution Ellen Barker had made to the meeting, and Rebecca had to admit that she had chosen her moment well.

'I realise that you are already working to capacity in your department, and I'm not exactly sure, yet, how the trial will affect you in the long run.' Rebecca paused a moment, tucking a stray strand of coppery hair behind her ear while she gathered her thoughts.

'Initially, though, it could have the effect of lightening your load slightly as some of the long-term problems like, for example, stiff necks and frozen shoulders were referred for evaluation. If a similar proportion of these respond as well to treatment as those in the first trials, it should result in an appreciable shortening of your waiting list.'

Ellen Barker was nodding her approval when Rebecca was interrupted.

'That still leaves you with the problems of lack of space in the department.' The pithy comment broke into her explanation but only served to give her impetus.

'Not at all.' She was hard pressed not to sound triumphant. 'In actual fact, it will have the effect of easing that situation, too, as the patients will be seen at my practice.'

'No!' he barked adamantly. 'Absolutely not.'

'I beg your pardon?' Rebecca was stunned. 'How else am I to see the patients? They have to come to my clinic to be examined and, if appropriate, start their treatment.'

'No,' he repeated, slightly more calmly this time. 'I cannot allow that. The patients will be treated here, under supervision.'

'I see.' Rebecca could hear for herself how icily calm her own voice had become—the lull before the storm, did he but know it. 'And where in your briefing does it say that you will be supervising my work? Where does it imply that my expertise is to be a subsidiary of yours? No!' She prevented him from interrupting. 'It is *my* turn to tell *you* what will be happening. These trials have been set up on the basis that we are all three complementary to each other, all with their own parts to play. As individuals we are each fully qualified to carry out our work without supervision.

'What has to be decided between the three of us,' she continued forcefully, 'is which categories of patients will have to be excluded from the trials. Only then will we be in a position properly to randomise the patient selection for the different forms of treatment.'

Rebecca found that she was shaking all over with the stress of controlling her anger, knowing that the heat in her cheeks was a clear indication of her heightened emotions. She flicked her tongue out quickly to moisten her lower lip, aware suddenly that he had watched her do it when his eyes followed the movement, darkening slightly as his pupils enlarged in response.

For several long moments there was silence, then, visibly gathering his thoughts, Alexander Marshall replied.

'I realise that it could create an impossible increase in workload for both the hospital and the staff involved. But, until I see how the system works out, I would not be happy to abrogate my responsibility towards the patients. They have been referred here in good faith by their GPs.

'I therefore propose,' he continued, his deep voice impossibly smooth, 'that, initially, we set up the scheme with patients being referred to a special clinic here, at the hospital. After a mutually agreeable time, we could then decide whether the system needed changing.'

He sat back again and propped one elbow on the arm of his chair to stroke the pen he held in one lean hand against the fullness of his lower lip. He stopped abruptly when, catching the direction of Rebecca's gaze, he apparently realised what he was doing.

Now it was Rebecca's turn to gather her thoughts away from her contemplation of the enticing perfection of a very masculine mouth, and she was grateful for the intrusion of Ellen Barker's voice.

'As an interim measure, that sounds like a good idea, but I shall be really interested to see how things progress. It would be wonderful to see some of my 'no-hope' patients finally having something else to try with even an outside chance of success.' She smiled wryly as she continued, 'of course that still leaves us with the problem of sorting out a timetable, and I've another meeting to attend this morning.'

'Would it be a good idea if I phoned you when I got back to my practice?' Rebecca suggested, relieved that the physiotherapist, at least, seemed to be going into the trials with a reasonably open mind. 'We could then sort out a list of possible times to fit in with Mr Marshall's timetable?' She glanced over at him, one surprisingly dark eyebrow raised questioningly.

'That would seem the most logical solution,' he agreed quietly. 'After that, we will just have to see how things go,' and his lean, powerful hands made short work of gathering up his papers ready to depart.

Rebecca was just following the physiotherapist out of the door when his deep voice called her back.

'I think it's important that we get the framework of this set up as quickly as possible. Have you any time free this afternoon?' Once again he was calm and in control, so much so that it almost made Rebecca doubt the evidence that she remembered seeing with her own eyes; the evidence that he was not quite as impervious to her as he would have her believe.

'I'm sorry, but I haven't any time free at all today.' She was surprised to find that she was genuinely sorry. It would have been a chance to speak to him without others being present, a chance to learn something about the man behind the stony façade. 'I had to leave the morning free for this meeting, which means I have a full afternoon of patients, and then I'm due out this evening.' She stopped hurriedly, aware that she was talking too much about things he had no need to know.

'I'm out this evening, too, so I'll have to get my receptionist to phone you to set up a meeting.' He paused as if he was going to continue the conversation, then shook his head slightly and raised his hand in a brief farewell as they parted company at the door.

'I'm glad that part of the evening's over.' Rebecca's father muttered in an aside. 'Now that I've sung for my supper, I'm free to enjoy myself!'

'Thomas! You shouldn't say things like that. It was a very important donation, and they had to have someone important to receive it for the sake of the publicity.'

'I know, Louise, I know, but sometimes I feel like a performing monkey at these "do"s.'

Rebecca smiled to herself as she heard her parents' quiet conversation. She felt rather the same way about this sort of function herself, especially as she was always on edge, waiting for the usual clash of wills with her father. It had been bad enough when she had lived at home, but when she was in company such as this it was almost inevitable.

The other guests at their table had been the usual mix of exalted colleagues and donating dignitaries, and there had been an intermittent stream of visitors arriving from the other tables to be introduced.

Rebecca felt the tingle on the back of her neck which indicated the presence of another person behind her chair, and waited for the introductions to begin.

This time her father's reaction was far from routine. With a broad smile on his face, he rose from his seat to shake their visitor's hand.

'Alexander, my boy. I see you got roped in, too. Good to see you. Have you met my wife? She's on the ENT team here.'

All Rebecca's senses sprang to attention the second she heard that unmistakable voice, and she held herself rigid so as not to betray any reaction.

'Pleased to meet you at last, Mrs James.'

'Louise, please, Alex. I'm sure we're going to see a great deal of each other, especially as you and Thomas now work in the same department.'

Rebecca must have made some small sound because her mother suddenly remembered she was there. 'I'm sorry. I'm forgetting my manners. May I introduce our daughter, Rebecca.'

With the awful sense that control of her life had been completely taken out of her hands, Rebecca turned in her seat to look up into the startled grey eyes of Alexander Marshall.

In a business suit he had looked powerful. In evening clothes he was downright lethal. The light gleamed over the unruffled perfection of his hair. His skin was burnished, his posture erect. He looked tough, confident, and unapologetically masculine.

'Mr Marshall and I have already met, Mother. Several times.' She held out her hand and when it was surrounded by the warm power of his she was glad she had remained sitting in her chair. The force of her unexpected reaction to his touch was stronger than ever, so much so that she was unaware that he was still holding her hand until several moments later when he gently deposited it on the arm of her chair.

A slight smile touched his face as he held her gaze effortlessly.

'Unfortunately, so far only in the line of work.' He was obviously answering a question put by one of her parents, and the realisation that she hadn't even heard the question snapped her back to reality.

'Work?' Her father queried. 'You don't mean you're tangled up in that nonsense she's involved in, do you?'

Here we go again, Rebecca thought wearily. Six years of this constant denigration so far, and how many more to come?

'Not directly.' His expression was slightly puzzled, as if he had wandered inadvertantly into uncharted lands. 'We have discovered we have some patients in common,' he continued discreetly, 'which means a certain amount of contact is inevitable.'

'Inevitable?' Her father scoffed brusquely. 'Just tell the misguided fools to stop wasting their time and money on charlatans!' He glared at Rebecca balefully until his wife discreetly placed her hand on his sleeve. 'Well,' he huffed, 'I still don't see why she couldn't have trained properly. It's not as if we couldn't have arranged a place for her at any medical school in the country if she didn't want to be right under our noses.'

'That wasn't the point, though, was it?' Rebecca was finally unable to continue biting her tongue. 'You were willing put yourself out to pull all sorts of strings, but only if I did what you wanted me to.' She had not consciously been aware how much of her hurt was revealed in her voice, and was amazed to hear the conciliatory tone in Alexander Marshall's words.

'Medicine isn't the career for everyone, is it?' She was startled to feel the warm weight of his hand descend on her shoulder and squeeze gently. 'Apart from the fact that most people couldn't stand the life, there's the basic fact that many who would love it can't get there because they aren't able to pass enough exams to be offered a chance to train.'

For several seconds Rebecca was too stunned to speak, then in one seamless movement she pushed her chair back from the table and rose to her feet, shrugging his hand off her shoulder furiously.

'How *dare* you patronise me?' she hissed, her nails digging into the palms of her hands as she clenched her fists with rage. 'How *dare* you assume that my choice of career is merely second-best—because I didn't "make the grade" to get into medical school.' She became aware out of the corner of her eye that her mother was making frantic signals, but shut them firmly out of her mind.

'Just how well qualified do you think a candidate should be before they are offered a place in such a hallowed institution?' she continued furiously. 'Would fourteen O levels and five A levels be bright enough?'

Suddenly she was aware that her words had fallen into an awful pool of silence; that their table was once again the centre of attention for the whole room.

Mortified at the spectacle she had just made of herself, she turned and, muttering a totally unintelligible apology, tried to push her way past the impressive frame of Alexander Marshall.

Only it didn't work. Not only did he not move aside but, when she tried to sidestep him, he moved, too.

'Let me pass,' she choked, her throat too tight for normal speech. If she didn't get out of this room soon, she was going to disgrace herself even further by bursting into tears.

'Certainly, if you want to give everyone watching the confirmation they need that something has happened here.' His voice was as low-pitched as hers and wouldn't have travelled to the ears of any of their companions in spite of the unnatural silence in the room.

She dared to glance up at him, knowing that her eyes would still show the telltale brightness of tears.

'Well, what's the alternative? Sitting at the table and listening to yet another tongue-lashing from my father about what a disappointment I am to them?'

'Actually, I was thinking you could dance with me.' A devilish smile lit up his eyes and started a strange melting sensation around her heart which she fought back.

'Dance? With you? Why?'

'Because there is music playing in the next room, because I want the chance to apologise to you without an audience, but most of all because I *want* to dance with you.' He held her gaze for long seconds then took possession of her hand.

'If you will excuse us,' he directed his words towards her parents, but they were clearly audible to their companions, 'Rebecca and I are going through to the other room to dance.'

As smooth as silk, he turned her away from the table. Her hand still gently imprisoned in his, she felt his other arm circle her so that his hand came to rest on the bare skin revealed by the back of her forest-green velvet dress, causing a tingle to run the length of her spine.

It took her eyes several seconds to adjust to the softer lighting in the other room, and by that time she found herself held loosely in his grasp, moving easily to the rather sedate music generally favoured during this part of the evening.

Darts of heat radiated from each point of contact until she felt that she was surrounded by his aura of warmth and power.

A small voice in the back of her mind struggled to make itself heard. This was the man who had deni-grated her and her profession from the moment they had met, and now he had been a witness to the same attitude from her own father.

While she was grateful for the way he had extricated her from her father's presence, that did not give him the right to propel her on to the dance floor in such a proprietorial manner.

She was startled to find that, while she had been fighting her inner battle, her hands must have crept up the front of his silky white shirt, because they were now clasped together at the back of his neck just high enough to feel the tickle of his well-groomed dark hair.

Unclasping her hands, she brought them down to wedge them between their bodies, flattening her palms against his chest so that she could look up into his face.

'What did you want to say?' She was having trouble sorting out her words, her thoughts were far too centred on the amazing heat which seeped into her hands to spread rapidly up her arms.

'Pardon?' Strangely, he seemed to be having an equal problem with communication.

'You said that you wanted to come in here to apologise. Why? I mean, what for?'

'I also said I wanted to dance with you.' He tightened his grasp across her back and tried to bring their bodies closer, but she resisted. She was discovering that the closer they were, the less her brain seemed able to work.

'All right, then. If you won't dance, perhaps I'd better make my apologies first,' and he led her to a heavily curtained alcove which concealed a doorway out on to a terrace.

The night air struck chill after the warmth of the room and she shivered. Before she could turn to re-enter the warm room, she was enveloped by the dark protection of his jacket. As she felt the slither of silky lining against the bare flesh of her shoulders she was also surrounded by the slightly musky tang which belonged only to the owner of the jacket.

She made a convulsive movement to slide it off, to escape the tantalising warmth and aroma, but his hands were too fast and held the lapels together under her chin.

'Please. You'll be too cold without it, and I need to speak to you.'

Rebecca went still. There was no way she could fight him; he was so much bigger and stronger, and seemed quite determined.

'What did you want to speak about? My unexpectedly illustrious background? That always gives everyone a shock. Two highly respected specialists with a traitor for a daughter. What a shame!'

'Stop it!' He shook her, one hand clasping each shoulder. 'That's not what I wanted to say at all.'

'Well, then?' Her tone was belligerent as she fought his attraction.

'I wanted to apologise for jumping to conclusions the way I did.'

'You're not the first, and I doubt you'll be the last.' Her combative air died as he reminded her of their dispute in front of so many people. 'My father doesn't help matters. He never misses the chance to make sure everyone knows what a disappointment I am to them.'

'If that's the case, why did you come with them this evening? You did have another offer.' His half-smile showed in the darkness as a gleam of teeth as he reminded her of his invitation.

'I was dreading this so much that I was almost tempted to accept.' She heard his soft laughter as the barb went home. 'But when Mother declares a command performance, it's much less wearing to obey, even if it does usually end up as unarmed combat.' She tilted her head back to see his expression and caught a peculiarly intent look on his shown up by the reflected gleam of light through the partly drawn curtains.

For endless seconds the glitter of his eyes held her trapped like a deer in the beam of headlights before his head slowly lowered towards hers.

She could have moved. At the very least, she could have turned her face away from him, but she hesitated just a fraction too long and it was too late.

The first contact was soft, a gentle brushing lighter than a moth's wing which left her light-headed with the need for more.

He caught her lower lip between his own, sampling, tasting before his tongue flickered out to stroke moisture along its fullness.

He paused briefly and she forced open heavy lids to try to focus on the gleam of moisture left on his own mouth.

She licked her lips, tasting his dark essence there, and heard him groan in response before he took her mouth in a kiss of stunning power. For long moments they were lost in each other, unable to tell or care where one of them ended and the other began.

He broke away from her, his breathing heavily uneven and muttered hoarsely as he clasped his hand behind her head to angle it for complete access.

'Mmm?' Rebecca mumbled distractedly before their mouths could fuse. 'What did you say?'

'What?' His eyes were focused totally on the lush perfection of her kiss-swollen lips.

'You said something.' Rebecca was rapidly losing interest in whatever he had said, impatient for him to kiss her again.

'I said, what a waste. . .' The words trailed away as

he concentrated on the softly pouting shape her mouth made.

Instantly, Rebecca stiffened. 'What a. . .'

She slammed both fists against his chest and when the shock caused him to loosen his grip she whirled out of his grasp.

'A waste, is it? So much for your apology. I should have known better.'

'Rebecca.' He almost sounded confused. 'What on earth is the matter with you?' He reached both hands towards her shoulders but she twisted, leaving him holding his own jacket.

At the threshold she turned to face him long enough to deliver the sentences which her disappointment demanded.

'You and my parents seem well matched. You all seem to think my career is a waste, but you've all forgotten something very important. I didn't choose chiropractic as a career to please anyone else but myself. The only thing that matters is that *I* am happy with my choice—and I am.' She turned sharply and entered the room, conscious that he was following closely behind.

She was aware out of the corner of her eye that he was shrugging into his jacket, and noticed that this had been remarked by several others, too.

Intending to track her parents down and see if they were ready to leave, she was hailed by her mother.

'Rebecca, I'm glad I found you at last. Your father's waiting for me with the Simminses. They've invited us back with them for a nightcap.' She glanced at her watch. 'It's not too late yet. Do you want to join us, or do you want to stay on here a bit longer and then get them to organise a taxi?'

'No, Mother. I'm ready to go home now, so I'll get that taxi straight away.'

'I'll see her home, Louise.'

'Oh, good. . .'

'No. . .' Rebecca gasped at his gall, but was unable to object before he continued.

'You go and find Thomas. I'll make sure she's safe.'

Within seconds Louise James had departed, leaving a seething Rebecca to explode.

'Safe, with you?' she scorned. 'I'm not going anywhere with you.' She made to turn away, but found her wrist held in a grip of steel.

'I told your mother I would see you home.' The pleasant companion had disappeared. There was no sign of warmth in his icy grey eyes now. 'If you weren't so intent on having a childish tantrum, you would see the sense of having company at this time of night.'

'Company. . .?'

'Don't worry,' he continued inexorably. 'I'm no keener than you are for us to spend any more time together than necessary, so let's get this over with,' and he led her through to collect her wrap and evening-bag.

The journey was a frozen nightmare, with each of them sat staring out of their respective side windows. Rebecca was furious with herself to realise that she was totally aware of every move he made, while he. . .? He seemed supremely indifferent to her presence.

Eventually, the taxi drew up outside her house.

Rebecca opened the door and stepped out. She was surprised, when she turned to close the door and pay her fare, to find that he had followed her out.

He muttered a brief word to the cabbie then, before Rebecca could utter more than a startled squeak, grasped her firmly by the elbow and marched her across to her front door.

'What do you think you're doing.' She had finally caught her breath and turned to berate him, fists planted on her hips.

'This. . .' He jerked her towards him, his arms sliding around her to pull her body into intimate contact with his before his head lowered to take her lips in a devastating kiss.

For Rebecca, even as angry as she was, it ended too soon.

'I don't know what your problem is——' his voice was darkly husky, the warmth of his breath shivering over her face as he spoke '—but it definitely disappears as soon as you stop talking and rely on your other senses.' His arms dropped to his sides, leaving her feeling abandoned, then he tipped her a sardonic salute and returned to the taxi.

'Why, you. . .you patronising, chauvinistic. . . beast!' she called after him in a venom-filled voice as soon as she had caught her breath. But he had closed the door and the taxi was drawing away, leaving her to fume alone.

It wasn't until she was curled into her bed that she remembered how closely she and Alexander Marshall were going to be working over the next few months.

She was suddenly aware that, for all the stunning attraction which sparked between them like an electric storm, she was dreading the next time they met. She had given him a whole arsenal of ammunition which he could use against her in their future battles.

CHAPTER THREE

PHYLLIS MARSHALL had responded well to her first session of treatment, and Rebecca was ashamed to find herself feeling rather smug. Even though her son had not accompanied her this time, Rebecca knew that his mother would certainly have let him know how she was progressing.

'So, put that in your pipe and smoke it!' she muttered under her breath, then pulled herself up short. She would do neither herself nor her patient any good if she persisted in gloating over the speed of Mrs Marshall's recovery. After all, it was not just down to her skill. There were many factors which could govern it, not least the patients' willingness to follow directions and their compliance with a suggested exercise regimen.

But oh, it did feel good to know that if, as he had warned, he was keeping a close eye on his mother's progress '—or otherwise', he couldn't have failed to notice the improvement.

The second point at which her life was overlapping that of Alexander Marshall was the feasibility trials and, much to her amazement, everything seemed to be running smoothly there, too.

Granted, she had not needed to speak to him personally, his secretary having handled the arrangement of mutually agreeable times for the meetings at the hospital, but she had been aware of a conflict within herself.

One part of her was glad not to have had to deal

with him herself. It was too soon after their disastrous confrontation for her to have any confidence that she would be able to control her temper. The other part of her was surprised at her vague feeling of emptiness—a hollow space inside her which she had not known existed before.

She was therefore only partly prepared for the jolt she felt right through her system when she found him waiting in the reception area after his mother's treatment session.

Once again he was impeccably dressed—did the man never relax in casual clothes?—and his face was as expressionless as it had ever been. Seeing him like this, it would be impossible to imagine the difference teasing laughter could make, unless you had seen it happen.

'Mr Marshall.' Rebecca acknowledged his presence formally. 'Did you want to speak to me, or have you just come to take your mother home?'

'Both.' He sounded a little taken aback by her tone, and paused briefly before continuing in an uncharacteristically hesitant way, 'I wondered if. . .if it would be convenient. . .' He shook his head in annoyance and continued in his more customary tone, 'Would you allow me to spend some time in your clinic on observation?'

Rebecca was startled by the sudden request. It was so totally unexpected. Did this mean he was becoming more open-minded about her profession, or. . .?

'Why?' Perhaps bluntness would get the answers she needed.

'Why? Well, I would have thought it would be obvious why. If I'm going to be agreeing to patients who have been referred to my department's being sent here, I must know what sort of thing I'm sending them to.'

It sounded all too logical, but Rebecca had the feeling that he was not telling her the whole story. Especially when she tried to read his eyes and found their expression totally shuttered against her.

Only time would tell if he had an ulterior motive.

'Very well, then. When would you like to come in?' She moved over to her appointment book. 'As you probably know by now, I will soon be leaving Tuesdays and Thursdays free to be at St Augustine's ready for when we get everything up and running, but I am in the practice here on Mondays, Wednesdays and Fridays.'

'Would it be inconvenient if I were to come back this afternoon, after I've dropped my mother back home?' His glance swept the open page. 'I see you've several patients due then.' He raised his head and she was held mesmerised by the silvery gleam in his eyes. 'Then I could take you for a meal afterwards.'

He must have seen the shock hit her as his suggestion registered, but he continued calmly, 'To discuss any questions I may have about your techniques and the principles behind them.'

He knew she had been about to refuse and had used the one argument she could not counter without damaging her credibility. How could she possibly object to his willingness to learn more about what she was doing?

Thinking fast, she made an alternative suggestion.

'That could be a little difficult for me, as I may have X-rays to develop after a new patient.' She tapped her bottom lip with one slender finger as if considering the options, and suddenly realised that his eyes had been riveted by the action. Whipping her hand away, she tried to quell the deep tremor which had started inside her as the memory of his kiss swept over her, and knew by the darkening of his eyes that he was remembering, too.

'I could meet you somewhere at about eight?' She cursed the slight quiver she heard in her voice.

'No, it would be better if I collected you. . .' he broke off as his mother entered the room, and was silent while she arranged her next appointment, leaving Rebecca fuming impotently at his high-handedness.

As he escorted his mother to the door, he paused at the last minute to toss back at her, 'I'll see you later this afternoon, then, and you can tell me where you would like to go this evening.' His eyes were full of devilment as he closed the door on her spluttered attempts at denial.

It was an unnerving experience, having the imposing figure of Alexander Marshall in the treatment-room while she was seeing her patients.

He had arrived just moments before the first patient was ready, confounding her hope that he would magically forget to come.

She had almost given herself indigestion worrying about the logistics of the situation, but had finally decided to stick to her usual routine of asking for the patient's permission for him to observe.

In the event, all her worrying and decision-making had been just so much wasted effort as he took the initiative right out of her hands.

'Mrs Potter,' he greeted the lady with a friendly smile and an outstretched hand, 'I'm Mr Marshall from the Orthopaedic department at St Augustine's. Dr James and I are working together on a project, and I was hoping you would allow me to be a fly on the wall while she is treating you?'

Some fly, Rebecca scoffed silently, as she watched

him charming her elderly patient effortlessly. It was a foregone conclusion that she was going to let him stay.

For the rest of the afternoon he was there, almost at her elbow.

It was not that he was interrupting or interfering, but his charm was such that each patient was unable to resist including him in the conversation, and inviting his comments and input on their condition.

'Well,' as one middle-aged businessman commented slyly, 'it's not every day you get the chance of a free consultation with a top orthopaedic surgeon!'

He had been one of the few who had thought to ask about Alexander Marshall's status, and had asked pertinently, 'Are you here to check up on Dr James, or are you hoping to pick her brains?'

Rebecca had looked across at the figure apparently relaxing in the chair she had positioned beside her desk, and raised one eyebrow at him.

'Perhaps it's a bit of both,' he conceded at last. 'It's not a field I've had a great deal of contact with in the past, and it's become necessary for me to find out exactly what the chiropractic sphere of expertise encompasses. Then we will know what benefit this can offer within the general run of medical care.'

'You mean chiropractic available on the NHS?' the patient queried hopefully.

'Who knows?' he shrugged. 'It's too early yet to predict what the outcome of the trials will be.'

That was a nicely non-committal answer, Rebecca thought.

It was not until she caught the wry smile lurking at the corner of his mouth that she realised her thoughts must have been mirrored on her face. Immediately she tried to erase the expression, but his brief shake of the head and the gleam which appeared in his eyes told her she had not been successful.

With each patient, he had started by asking the same basic questions. Why had they decided to come to a chiropractor? Why had they not gone to their GP?

Several patients had been rather reticent, as if afraid to upset him, but others were more open.

It was an apparently meek and mild housewife who was the most forthcoming.

'I did go to my doctor first, but after weeks and weeks of being put off with prescriptions for drugs which did little or nothing to help, I got fed up, and tried to pin him down.'

'What do you mean?' Alexander sounded genuinely puzzled.

'I asked him point-blank if he had made a diagnosis or if he was just chasing symptoms with a variety of drugs in the hope that either the problem would go away, or I would!'

For several seconds there was silence, then all three of them burst out laughing.

'What did he say?' Rebecca was the first to recover her breath.

'Not a lot,' she said drily. 'Oh, he huffed and puffed a lot, but what it all came down to was that I was asking a plumber to play with the electrical system!'

Once again there was a gust of laughter at this particularly telling witticism.

'I take it you have some connection with the building trade?' Alexander queried, still smiling.

'Well, it just seems to make sense to me when I look at it that way,' she replied. 'As Dr James explained on my first visit, if there was something wrong with the chemical side of my body, like cancer, for example, then I would need chemicals to help sort it out. But if it's the mechanical side that isn't working, then it makes sense to me that it needs a more mechanical type of treatment.' She paused and flushed slightly. 'I'm sorry if I sound as if I'm some sort of fanatic, but this is the first time in months that I've felt well.

'It makes me mad that my GP couldn't be honest with me and tell me I'd be better off going to a chiropractor. After all,' she challenged, 'GPs have been permitted to refer patients to them for years. Unfortunately, mine was so narrow-minded he hadn't even bothered to find out about them.' She looked across at Alexander Marshall. 'Thank goodness there are some specialists, like you, who have finally seen the light. Hopefully, this means fewer people will get to the end of their tether before they find out for themselves that they can get help.'

That's what you think, Rebecca commented wryly to herself, this time making sure that she was not facing him, but nevertheless sure that he would know what she was thinking.

'So what *was* the problem?' He turned to Rebecca suddenly. 'What did you find that her GP missed?'

Rebecca heard the challenge in his tone, knew he was fully prepared to scoff. She was just grateful that her patient hadn't sensed his attitude.

'Mrs Wilkens was suffering from migraine-type headaches.'

'But there are so many different treatments for that. It could just have been a case of hitting on the right one for her.'

'Except that her doctor had completely discounted the fact that Mrs Wilkens had never suffered from migraine headaches before she had a shunt accident in her car.'

'And. . .?' His eyes pierced her like steely points.

'And, as soon as her neck was treated——'

'The very first time, too,' her patient interrupted eagerly.

'—the headaches stopped.' Rebecca finished simply.

'Any recurrence?'

'One episode——'

'Ahh!' he broke in, but Rebecca continued, undeterred.

'—when she had an argument with some curtains while trying to hang them up.'

'What she means is that I was an idiot,' Mrs Wilkens admitted wryly. 'I was feeling so much better that I started spring-cleaning. I tried to put the curtains up myself and slipped on the ladder. I didn't fall, but I wrenched my shoulder hanging on.'

'So, what treatment have you been giving her?' he demanded. 'Heat and massage? A cervical collar?'

'None of them!' Rebecca was aware of the horror in her tone. 'I believe collars have a very limited use. They prevent the normal use of the neck.'

'Surely that's the whole point? To prevent further damage?'

'Except that the resulting lack of use weakens the whole neck. When the collar is finally removed, the neck is more vulnerable to injury than ever, unless the patient has had the benefit of physiotherapy in the interim. And we all know how short of time those departments are.'

'What is your alternative?' Rebecca thought his tone was slowly becoming more neutral—or was that wishful thinking?

'I found that some of the vertebrae in her neck were not moving properly. The muscles had gone into protective spasm.' She glanced at him, her expression reminding him of his mother's similar problem, although patient confidentiality meant that she couldn't mention the fact in front of her present patient.

'Once I had freed them up,' she continued, 'I showed Mrs Wilkens some isometric exercises to do to strengthen her neck and help to prevent a recurrence.'

This time he made no comment, merely nodding his understanding of her explanation.

Rebecca completed the treatment session, her heart lifting at the thought that maybe, just maybe, he was starting to listen to what she was saying. Maybe he was starting to realise that there were enormous benefits to the inclusion of chiropractic expertise into the NHS.

By the end of the afternoon there had still been no time for Rebecca to initiate a discussion about their proposed 'meeting' later that evening, and she was furious to discover a note on her desk when she finished taking X-rays of her final patient.

'So, he's sorry he had to leave without saying good-bye but will pick me up at eight as arranged!' she fumed, and half of her was tempted to take herself off somewhere so that he arrived at an empty house.

The saner side of her mind realised that although the arrangement felt disturbingly like a date, there was no reason why she should not insist that they discuss business, as he had originally suggested.

Even though you'd rather he had asked you out just for your company, a little voice whispered in her ear, and was promptly silenced.

She had intended dressing casually, as a welcome relief from her professional appearance throughout the day. Then she remembered that she had never seen Alexander Marshall in anything remotely casual, even when he was acting as chauffeur for his mother.

A quick shuffle through her wardrobe showed her

that she had few items which bridged the gap between ultra-smart business wear and jeans, without resorting to the cocktail-dress type of outfit which her mother had insisted on buying for her to wear when she went out with her parents.

The only thing which seemed remotely suitable was a pair of black trousers in a fine, flowing wool, the fabric pleated on to a wide waistband to give the effect of a cummerbund, teamed with a cream silk shirt. She knew she would look elegant enough for almost any destination without looking overdressed.

The quiet purr of a silver-grey BMW announced his arrival at exactly eight, and she stepped out of the door immediately, having decided that this approach would set the businesslike atmosphere for the evening.

'You're very prompt,' she commented brightly in an attempt to set the tone of the evening. Her plan was spoiled slightly when he insisted on opening the passenger door for her to settle her into the car.

'You look stunning,' he murmured, as he leant towards her, surrounding her with a subtle hint of spice.

So do you, she thought, as she watched him circle the front of the car. Not a suit this time, but a sports jacket that looked as if it was made of Harris tweed and a pair of dark trousers. His cream shirt looked like the masculine twin to her own, but was teamed with a silk tie with a subtly woven Paisley design.

'Do you have any preferences as to where we go?' he asked as he started the engine. 'Or are you willing to trust me?'

'Trust you?' There was a challenge in the quizzical lift of her eyebrow.

'To decide where we're going.' There was just enough inflection in his voice to tell her that he was enjoying their banter, and Rebecca was surprised to discover that she was enjoying it, too.

They were not travelling long before he drew into the car park of a pub with a well-deserved reputation for the excellence of the meals served in the attached four-star restaurant.

'Does this meet with your approval?' he enquired politely, and Rebecca was pleased to agree wholeheartedly.

'I vaguely remember hearing that they won some award or other.' She smiled up at him as he insisted on helping her out of the car.

Once inside, they were quickly seated at a table for two in a secluded alcove, and Rebecca realised that the table must have been booked in advance. Primed to make a comment, she suddenly remembered to bite her tongue. This was to be a dignified business meeting, and the isolation of the table would probably be an asset, especially if the discussion turned towards their differing ideologies.

He shifted in his seat, and Rebecca's eyes were drawn once again to the breadth of his shoulders. She had never really thought about it before, but now she supposed that his work in orthopaedic surgery must require a great deal of strength and stamina.

She found that she wanted to know what form of sport or other exercise he took to keep himself in such superb condition and, when she came to ask the question, suddenly realised that she didn't know how to address him.

The irony of the situation made her chuckle, drawing his attention.

'Was it good enough to share?' he asked, making her laugh again.

'Actually, I was just thinking of asking you a question and I realised I don't know what to call you.' She grinned at his puzzlement, and explained, 'When you're at St Augustine's, you're Mr Marshall, the consultant orthopaedic surgeon. When you're accompanying your mother, I hear her calling you Alexander, but what should you be called in this sort of venue?'

His eyes lit up as he, too, saw the humour of the situation.

'Alex,' he said, with a slightly husky tone to his deep voice, and his eyes darkened as they caught hers. 'Just Alex.' He held her gaze for several seconds before asking, 'And you?'

Rebecca found she had to clear her throat before her voice would emerge.

'Well, you know my name is Rebecca. My friends call me Becca.'

'Do I qualify?' he queried quietly, and she found herself nodding silently as their waitress arrived.

The meal which followed was excellent, made all the more so by the conversation which flowed, surprisingly easily, between them.

By the time their coffee was served, Rebecca was feeling decidedly guilty for avoiding any and all mention of work—not that Alex seemed worried.

Alex.

It seemed strange to be able to call him that when, if she was honest with herself, she had been thinking of him as Alex almost from the first time she heard his name—in spite of the fact they had hardly managed to hold a civil conversation until tonight.

The rich depths of his voice broke into her musings.

'At the risk of upsetting the peace, what *did* make you decide to become a chiropractor?'

'You mean, instead of becoming a *real* doctor?'

'Not in that way, I don't, so smooth down your ruffled fur!' he admonished. 'I was more interested in your reasons, your motivation; they must have been pretty strong, going on what little I've seen of the opposition you had.'

'You're right about the opposition!' Rebecca shook her head. 'You would have thought I had announced my decision to be a prostitute or a serial killer!'

'Joking aside, though, I would like to know.' His tone was quietly sincere, his gaze direct, and Rebecca found her throat closing up for a moment as tears came threateningly close.

'Do you know,' she finally managed in a shaky voice, 'my parents never asked me that. They never asked me *why*. They just condemned the idea out of hand and tried to browbeat me into submission.'

'Why did they assume that you would go into medicine in the first place?'

'Oh, *that* was ordained from the moment I was born.' She tried to speak airily, but heard for herself the little wobble. 'Of course, by then they'd had to come to terms with their first big disappointment—the fact that I wasn't the boy they wanted, especially as they'd decided they were only having one child.'

Shock stopped her speaking for a moment as his hand slid gently over hers in a gesture of silent support.

'We both know how hard it is to get into medical school; the hours of slog it takes to get the grades. So, if you were willing to put in all that effort, why did you change your mind at the last minute.'

'I didn't,' she said simply. 'Oh, I did work hard; you don't get that many good grades unless you do. And they always checked up on my grades.' She was briefly lost in memories. 'Sometimes it seemed to be the only way to get them to notice me. A poor report just

earned me a cold, "do better next time," but straight
As had them both thrilled. Not that they spent much
time with me—they were too busy.'

'So, how did chiropractic come into the picture?' He
nudged her back towards the original topic, and she
was suddenly aware of how much she had told him
about herself. She never spoke like this to anyone,
especially to someone who had showed such animosity
towards her profession.

'I'm sorry to have talked your ear off like that,' she
sidestepped his question clumsily. 'I must have sounded
like a real spoilt brat. Perhaps you'd better put it down
to the lateness of the hour.'

He shot back his cuff to consult the wafer-thin gold
watch nestled among the dark hairs on his tanned wrist.

'Are you sure you don't want another coffee?' At
her refusal, he signalled for the bill and within minutes
they were on their way.

Rebecca had expected him to drop the conversation,
but he seemed to find the dark confines of the car ideal
for quiet talk.

'I used to be very conscious of my background.' She
was surprised to hear the admission; he seemed so full
of confidence. 'It's hardly run-of-the-mill for choosing
medicine as a career, but at least we were a close
family, and I was allowed to decide what I wanted to
do.'

His voice was as resonant as ever in the plush luxury
of the car, and the darkness encouraged Rebecca to
answer.

'I thought I would be allowed to choose, too, in spite
of the fact that they were already talking about options
for eventual specialisation when I was only fifteen! I
thought it was just the sort of talk I heard in my

friends' homes, with various ideas being thrown around.'

She shook her head, ruefully.

'It was just after I was eighteen that I first found out about chiropractic. I was going to a sixth form college and one of the other pupils' father was a chiropractor. I had an accident while I was trampolining, and "whiplashed" my neck.'

'Didn't you tell your parents? What about your GP?' For the first time that evening she was aware of an unexpected edge to his voice.

'Oh, I told them, and while they were giving me a lecture about wasting time on the trampoline when I could have been studying they gave me a handful of tablets and a surgical collar.'

They pulled up smoothly outside her house and he reached up to switch on the courtesy light.

'Did you wear it?' The tension was still there.

'For about a week.' She met his gaze full-on and saw the knotting of the muscles in his jaw. 'The most miserable week of my life, and it did nothing to relieve the pain or the blinding headache. It also happened to be a particularly hot week, so I ended up with a heat rash, too!' She saw him wince and continued, 'I decided that anyone who could condemn a patient to one of those things should be made to wear it first!'

She gathered up her bag and wrap and he took the hint, coming round to walk her to the door, his hand at her elbow.

'You haven't finished the story,' he teased. 'How can you expect me to survive without hearing the happy ending?'

Rebecca, too, had been wishing that the evening did not have to end.

'I can take a hint.' She smiled, glad that his strange

mood seemed to have lifted. 'Did you want to come in for some coffee?'

'The coffee isn't essential. It's the company I'm enjoying.' His deep voice was sending shivers of arousal down her spine, and she was suddenly afraid that he would see the effect he was having on her.

Fumbling with the key, she quickly let them into the house and led the way to her kitchen.

Once she had put the coffee-pot on and set the tray she was left with nothing to do but wait, every nerve-end tingling with awareness.

She turned to find him leaning against the door-frame, watching her as closely as a cat watches a mouse just before it pounces.

Sheer tension took over and she rushed to continue the interrupted conversation.

'Anyway, to cut a long story short, I was due to stay with my friend that weekend as it was half-term break and my parents would both be working. When I walked in the door with that contraption on, the first thing his father asked was if I'd been X-rayed and then what treatment I was receiving.'

'As I was over eighteen, I was able to decide for myself that I wanted him to treat me, and in a matter of hours the headache had gone and within days the pain had gone too. He gave me similar exercises to do to strengthen my neck as I gave Mrs Wilkens today, and I've never had any further trouble.'

As she finished her story, she was all too aware that she had meant it to be a challenge, but instead of taking up the gauntlet he defused the situation by questioning her motives.

'So what was the final thing which pushed you into deciding you wanted it enough as a career to defy your parents?' His genuine interest had never wavered throughout her meandering tale, in spite of his odd bouts of tension.

'I think it was the realisation that I could be in charge.' She grinned at him and then clarified, 'Not like you are—sort of a team-leader who depends on everyone else to do their job so that you can do yours. With my job, I am the whole team. I examine the patient, take and read the X-rays, make the diagnosis, plan the treatment and perform it. When the patient finally finishes treatment, I feel such satisfaction. . .' She shook her head as she ran out of words, then decided to turn the tables on him.

'But what about you?' she queried. 'What on earth made you decide to slog yourself to get the grades?'

The coffee gurgled to a halt and Alex carried the tray through to the small table in front of her couch.

Rebecca kicked off her shoes and curled her feet under her as she sat down so that she was facing him and signalled for him to speak.

'Mine wasn't quite the blinding flash of realisation that yours was, but there are similarities. I had always wanted to be a doctor, ever since my father died as the result of an industrial accident.'

Rebecca made a soft sound of distress.

'The doctors fought hard for two years, but I often think that he died the day of the accident and just his shell was left.' A wealth of sorrow was in his words, and Rebecca leant forward to lay her hand over his in a spontaneous gesture of comfort.

He turned to her and their gazes fused, silver-grey to velvety brown, with an almost audible crackle. Flustered, Rebecca dropped her eyes to focus on their linked hands and heard his slightly husky voice pick up the story.

'I was about eighteen when I got my motorbike—

just like most of my classmates. It was a sort of status symbol, as was going into pubs. Unfortunately, some of them, like my friend, mixed the two. One day he came off his bike and went under a lorry.'

Rebecca gasped at the mental image, and her hand tightened briefly.

'He wasn't killed, but many times I heard him wish he had been—especially after each of his bouts of reconstructive surgery. The things the surgeons managed to do.' He shook his head in remembered amazement.

'He came very close to having one leg amputated, it was in such a mess; but they saved it by putting the jigsaw of bone together with screws and plates. Do you know——' a rogue grin lit up his face '—he's got so much metal in him that he sets off the metal detectors at airports!'

They exchanged a wry smile at the mental image conjured up.

'Anyway, I was so fascinated by what they were doing for him that my decision was made.'

'Is it very hard work? I mean, physically? Do you have to be in good shape or are you naturally. . .?' Rebecca stumbled to a halt and blushed furiously as she realised that her original thoughts had surfaced on the end of her tongue.

'You don't mind if I take that as a compliment, do you. . .whether you meant it as one or not?' He leant closer to her, using their clasped hands to draw her towards him. 'I like the thought that you've been looking at my body and wondering. It means that I can admit to doing the same about you.'

Each word caused a soft puff of air to stir the tendrils of coppery hair against her neck. A shiver of arousal travelled down her back and her eyelids began to feel heavy until all she could focus on was the chiselled perfection of his mouth.

'Becca.' For the first time she heard the diminutive of her name on his lips and her own parted in response, her eyes lifting languidly to meet the darkness of his.

'Becca.' He repeated it like a prayer, then paused, gritting his teeth briefly. 'I don't know what you're doing to me. I think you must be casting some sort of a spell.' He shook his head, then gave her hand a brief squeeze before releasing it to stand up. 'I don't think I'd better stay. It's starting to get late and we both have busy days tomorrow . . . No! Dammit! No social lies.' He stepped towards her and pulled her up out of her corner of the couch.

Without her shoes on she had to look a long way up to meet his eyes and what she saw there made her pulse race. No longer icy, his eyes now bore the heat of molten steel as they gazed down at her, the deep black of his pupils widely dilated with arousal.

The tip of her tongue came out to touch her lips and Alex groaned as he reached for her and wrapped his arms around her, surrounding her with his warmth and strength.

'You *are* a witch!' he murmured into her neck, his warm breath setting off a shiver of reaction. 'And the real reason I can't stay here is because I want to stay too much.'

His hands moved to her shoulders and he pushed on them to seperate their bodies just far enough so that they could see each other. 'I don't know what's happening between us. All I know is that it's happening fast and we need to slow it down.' He took a deep breath. 'We still have to work together and I don't want the two situations to. . .'

'I understand,' Rebecca soothed, amazed that she

was even capable of coherent speech. 'We'll take things slowly and find out where they lead us.'

'See me to the door?' he invited, releasing her shoulders and capturing her hand. 'Don't forget to lock up after me,' he reminded her as he turned towards her, then, 'Oh, hell! I can't. . .' And she was in his arms again, his head swooping down to cover her mouth in a devastating kiss.

Within seconds Rebecca was boneless with pleasure, and all sense of who or where she was receded as she responded ardently to every change of angle, every thrust of his tongue.

Long moments later they surfaced, each as breathless as the other and both leaning weakly against the front door.

'I must go.' His voice was husky with arousal. 'I knew I shouldn't touch you, but I couldn't resist.' He leant forward for a brief second, the contact between their lips the merest whisper of a promise. 'Don't forget to lock up,' he murmured as he finally turned away. 'I'll see you tomorrow afternoon.'

Rebecca had finished all her nightly chores and was curled up in bed when his parting words had her racing for her appointment book.

No, she didn't have a meeting with him tomorrow at St Augustine's, and his mother wasn't due for an appointment either.

Did that mean that he was going to come in to observe again, or did he mean he wanted to see her?

CHAPTER FOUR

ALEX finally arrived late in the afternoon. Rebecca had found herself listening for him and only the sternest of lectures to herself made her concentrate fully.

She had just shown in her final patient of the day: an elderly man who was waiting for an appointment for a hip operation.

'This one is just up your street,' she joked with Alex, having introduced him to the patient. 'Unfortunately, he still has some while to wait before it's his turn, and he has a problem with taking painkillers.'

'If it's a surgical problem, why is he coming to you?' Alex queried, his face becoming the mask she hoped had disappeared forever.

'For relief,' the patient butted in suddenly.

'What sort of relief?' Alex asked. 'Didn't you go back to your GP to see if he could change your prescription for something that suited you better?'

'Several times, but they all caused too many problems.' The poor man sounded resigned. 'In the end he sent another letter to the specialist telling him about my drug-intolerance problem and asking him to fit me in as soon as possible.'

'So, why are you coming here? What can a chiropractor do for you that your GP couldn't?' He sounded sceptical.

'Well, she treated a friend of mine when he was waiting for the same operation and he told me it was worth while coming to be shown how to cope with things while I wait.'

'What do you mean?'

'You'd do better to ask Doctor to explain. She'll make a better job of it than I will.' He smiled at her happily.

'So, what can you do for these cases?' Rebecca was startled to hear that he was barely managing to keep his tone civil, and the realisation gave her a nasty jolt.

It took determination for her to smile serenely at her patient while she gathered her thoughts.

'By the time patients with coxarthrosis reach the stage Mr Burgess has, it's been months or even years since they've walked properly and this often creates problems with the mechanics of the rest of the body.' She glanced up at Alex as he towered over her radiating disapproval and found that his total concentration was on her.

'Such as?' he challenged.

'Do you want the short answer or the detailed one?' she queried.

His raised eyebrow taunted her.

'As you know, pain often starts in one leg before the other. It's normal for patients to protect the painful leg by using the other one more—for example using it to go upstairs or to push up out of the chair. Unfortunately this can actually hasten the degeneration of the other leg.' She paused for a minute, thoughtfully.

'Stand on one leg,' she demanded suddenly.

'Pardon?'

'Stand on one leg. Bend the other knee. You can hold on to the back of a chair if you need. . .'

He snorted his disdain for her suggestion.

'Now what?'

'Look straight ahead into the mirror and tell me if your eyes are level—horizontally.'

'Of course they are.' He sounded mildly exasperated.

'Why do you say "of course"? You aren't standing level.' she challenged.

'No.' he agreed. 'The spine is compensating for the lifted leg.'

'And where this is long-term, it can cause uneven wear and tear. Similarly, it can cause problems with ligaments and muscles with overuse and disuse. Then, of course, there are circulatory problems because of lack of mobility.

'Last but not least are the psychological problems. Some patients are so affected by the physical break-down of their bodies that they've already given up, and their recovery rate will be poorer.'

'So what does your treatment do for them?'

'I can help to restore some of the mobility, which can also help to lessen the pain. I can also show the patient what sort of exercises will strengthen their muscles so that when they have their operation they will recover faster.'

'Apart from that, she nags us something rotten about all the bad habits we've got into!' Mr Burgess added. 'But I reckon it's worth the money it costs just to get some relief, even on a pension.'

'The other thing I sometimes suggest is that they might want to visit an acupuncturist,' Rebecca continued.

'Another alternative therapy.' His tone was suddenly icy with condemnation. 'Why?'

'Primarily for pain relief,' Rebecca kept her voice calm with an effort. Why was Alex sounding so utterly disapproving? A moment ago he had seemed far more. . .accepting.

Realising that she must continue, she took a breath to steady her voice.

'Particularly in a case such as this, where Mr Burgess

is in a lot of pain and has little prospect of relief.
Whether he decides to go to one or not is his decision.'

Rebecca hoped Mr Burgess hadn't heard the dispar-
aging snort Alex had made.

Turning her back on Alex, she concentrated on
treating her patient, praising him for the increased
suppleness he had achieved already, which was the
proof of his diligence with his exercise regimen.

'Well, Doctor, there's no point in paying for your
advice and then ignoring it!' he quipped, then commented in a man-to-man aside to Alex, 'I tell you, I
haven't had a woman make me sweat this much in
years!' and he chuckled his way out to get dressed.

Alex remained silent while Rebecca completed her
notes on the patient's file, and stayed in the treatment-
room when she went through into the reception area to
make Mr Burgess's next appointment.

When she finally returned to the treatment-room, he
was standing in what she had come to think of as 'his'
spot in the corner by the window. His arms were folded
across the breadth of his chest as he leant against the
wall, and his expression was forbidding.

Rebecca realised that in her absence his mood had
deteriorated badly as he hardly waited for her to enter
the room before he fired a broadside.

'Why are you playing pass-the-parcel with that poor
man?' The vehemence of his words was like a physical
attack.

'I beg your pardon?' Rebecca began but was not
allowed to continue.

'Who are you suggesting he sees? Do you all send
them around from one to the other of you until they
run out of money? Are these other people even qualified, or didn't you think to check?' he fired volley after

volley without pausing for breath until she finally broke in.

'How *dare* you?' Rebecca shrieked, totally incensed. 'How dare you even *think* that I would do anything so unethical as to send a patient for unnecessary treatment, let alone to someone without proper qualifications.'

She was shaking so much that she had to clasp her hands together tightly. 'Didn't you listen to anything I said yesterday? Haven't you even bothered to do some research into what we're trying to do, or are you too arrogant to admit that you don't know everything?'

Rebecca's anger was at white heat, but she was still able to see the flush which stained his cheekbones.

'And what about me?' She heard the slight crack in her voice, but ignored it. 'If that's the sort of person you think I am, why would you want to spend time with me—or was that just your hormones ruling your head?'

This time Rebecca saw all the colour drain from his face.

'No.' His voice was hoarse. 'No, it wasn't like that and you know it.'

'Do I?' Rebecca retorted bitterly. 'How do I know what to think when you can attack my integrity like this?' She drew in a deep, unsteady breath, and managed to control her voice. 'Do you really think I'm capable of cynically passing patients around to unqualified practitioners? You know how much my profession means to me—enough to cause a permanent rift in my family. Do you honestly think I would betray it like that?'

'I'm sorry.' In two strides he had reached her and tried to take her in his arms.

'Don't.' Rebecca stepped back sharply, refusing to allow him to touch her.

'I am sorry,' he dropped his arms to his sides and his shoulders lifted with the deep breath he took. 'I over-reacted badly and took it out on you.'

'Why?' she asked simply. 'Why react like that at all?'

'If you had seen some of the things I've seen, both during my training and in my personal life. . .' He shook his head. 'You'd be as suspicious as I am.'

'I know for a fact that I would not react the same way as you.' Rebecca retorted sharply. 'I would make sure of my facts before I attacked anyone's integrity like that.' Once again a tide of red stained his face as she continued.

'For your information, I have a list of properly qualified practitioners which I compiled when I set up practice. This includes the many branches of comple-mentary medicine as well as the more "orthodox" ones, including eminent orthopaedic surgeons.'

'Yes, well. . .' he tried, but she refused to allow him to speak.

'How would you like it if I were to suggest that you would refuse to see a patient who needed a hip replacement just because they had been referred by a chiropractor in the initial instance.'

He seemed to bristle with indignation. 'That would be totally unethical. It's the patient's welfare that matters, not petty politics.' He sounded appalled that she should believe otherwise.'

'I rest my case.' Rebecca folded her arms smugly.

'It's not the same thing at all. . .' Alex started to say until he saw her raised eyebrow, then he subsided.

'We each have our code of ethics, but central to all of them is the patient, isn't it?' Rebecca suggest crisply. 'As long as we are properly qualified and properly regulated, then all that's left is for us to learn to trust each other.'

She turned and walked away from him, her anger spent and a vaguely empty feeling left in its place.

'Are you free to come out for a drink this evening, Becca?' His voice was subdued. 'We need to talk, to spend time together.'

'I am free, but I'd rather not go out with you this time.' She shook her head when he started to speak. 'No, I'm not saying it to punish you. That would be childish, and when you know me better you'll know that my temper may be spectacular but I never bear a grudge.'

'Then, why won't you come out? How am I supposed to get to know you better if you won't see me?'

'I think we both need some time to think about the situation, Alex. To decide whether there's any point in trying to develop a relationship outside our professional contacts.' She gave a brief sigh. 'Maybe there are too many differences of attitudes and ideology for there to ever be anything more, but anyway I need time to think about it.'

'So you have decided and no one else gets a chance to put their opinion?' His voice and his eyes were both icy now.

'No. I'm just telling you how I see the situation. What my feelings are.' She tried running her fingers through her hair to relieve the tension headache which was threatening and encountered her neatly braided hair. 'Can we make some time in the future; set a date when we can get together to talk calmly. . .?'

'Fine.' He threw over his shoulder as his long legs took him swiftly towards the door. 'I'll get my secretary to contact you.'

'Well! He's certainly cornered the market in parting shots!' she muttered into the empty room.

It was several moments before the humour of the situation finally struck her. This was a man who projected an air of icy control, while underneath she was discovering a seething maelstrom of emotions.

In spite of her misgivings about their professional relationship, Alexander Marshall, the man, was becoming more intriguing by the day.

After their disagreement the night before, Rebecca was rather dreading the first major meeting the following afternoon at St Augustine's.

In the event, it entailed several hours of concentrated study of a huge pile of case-notes which all needed to be classified.

Expecting the copious quantities of dust which piles of paperwork seemed to generate, Rebecca had taken the precaution of dressing far more casually than normal and tying her hair back in a gleaming ponytail.

Ellen Barker was dressed similarly, her uniform nowhere in evidence, but it was Alex who took her breath away.

For the first time he too was informally dressed in a pair of jeans and a boldly checked shirt. The sleeves were rolled up to reveal the strength of his well-muscled forearms, their sprinkling of dark hair showing against the smoothly tanned skin.

Rebecca's pulse-rate rose suddenly and her mouth became dry as dust, especially when he merely tossed a general greeting as he entered the room.

In spite of her disappointment, Rebecca was totally aware of his presence in the room. She found herself glancing briefly in his direction each time she reached for the next file of case-notes, then feeling upset that he never seemed to be looking her way.

It was not until they reached the stage of cross-checking each others' findings that Rebecca realised that there was going to be a problem.

Her heart sank as she realised the enormity of what she had to say, but there was no alternative.

'Mr Marshall.' The situation called for total formality. 'I'm afraid there is a problem developing here that needs some further discussion.'

'Yes, Dr James? And what might that be?' His tone was coolly sardonic. 'Have you just realised the size of the task?'

'The size of the task is much as I expected, given that I intend my contribution to the trials to be faultless.' She kept her voice emotionless. 'The problem I'm referring to is the fact that you have been systematically disqualifying nearly sixty per cent of the possible subjects from even being considered for inclusion in the trials. And that's before we have formulated a policy for those categories which will have to be excluded.'

'Do you have a problem with the fact that I have used my clinical expertise to start the selection procedure? Do you doubt my qualifications for doing so?'

'I certainly don't doubt your degree of qualification. What I do object to is the fact that you have started making any selections at all!' She hung on to her composure by a mere thread, helped by the fact that she seemed to have rendered him speechless by her attack.

'If you continue to do this, you are jeopardising the validity of the whole trial, and I would have no alternative but to report to the trial organisers that any conclusions drawn from such biased premises would be null and void.' Rebecca kept her hands under the level of the table so that he could not see how badly they were shaking.

Why was he doing this? Was he deliberately trying to sabotage the trials? But that would be stupid as it would reflect so badly on his participation. Or, was it *her* presence which he was trying to alter?

'Mrs Barker, do you have a problem with this?' How smooth his voice was now.

'Well, Mr Marshall, I've actually found several problems.' Her tone was apologetic but firm. 'Firstly, I feel that if we are going to be working on this marathon for however many weeks and months, the most basic thing would be to drop all this "Mrs" and "Dr" business. My name is Ellen, and I'd like you both to use it.'

Rebecca and Alex looked sheepishly at each other. They both had the grace to recognise how petty their game of one-upmanship had been and agreed rapidly.

'Secondly, I agree with Rebecca that nothing we do in these early stages must jeopardise the trials, otherwise we'll all be wasting our time.' It was easy to see how she managed to keep on top of a busy department. She spoke totally to the point without fear or favour.

'Thirdly, although my input is important at various stages, initially, in this "exclusion" process, it is you two who have the degree of knowledge necessary to devise the formula. As I said before, it is essential that not only is it done correctly—for the sake of the patients—but it must be *seen* to be done correctly for the sake of the trials.'

She sat back and looked calmly from one to the other, for all the world like a headmistress with two unruly pupils.

Finally, Alex spoke. 'You're quite right, Ellen. We're lucky to have you to point out the obvious, although it shouldn't have been necessary in the first place. I hope we won't need your mediating services from now on.'

Ellen laughed. 'I would be most surprised if we didn't each have to take a turn as peacemaker from time to time. We're all rather opinionated people — that's probably why we were chosen for this in the first place.

'Now,' she continued, 'I think it's time for that great British institution, the tea break, before we really get stuck in,' and she swept out to organise a tray.

For long moments Rebecca and Alex sat in silence each gazing at the mountain of paperwork in front of them before they both spoke at once.

'I'm sorry. . .'

'I'm sorry. . .' Rebecca gave a wry grin and gestured for Alex to continue.

'I shouldn't have taken pot-shots at you like that, Becca. It was totally unprofessional to let my personal feelings run over into this.' He patted a pile of files.

'But very human.' Rebecca was looking at him and saw his start of surprise before he could disguise it.

'Alex, I understood why you were short with me when you arrived this morning. We didn't part on very good terms last night and it made things uncomfortable for both of us. That's one of the things we need to talk about later. But when it came to the trials, that was a different matter. I was willing to have the whole trial cancelled, in spite of what the publicity would have done to my career, rather than. . .'

'I agree entirely, Becca,' he broke in. 'But we are going to have a problem thrashing out this next stage. I can't see how we are ever going to agree on our terms of reference. At the moment everything is being clouded by our conflicting expectations. You can see your view of what should be happening, but in all conscience I can't abrogate my responsibilities. Heaven only knows how the other trials are coping with this.'

'That's it! You've got it!' Rebecca suddenly shot out of her seat, her face animated and her eyes shining. 'Oh, aren't we idiots?' She was smiling broadly.

'Speak for yourself,' he objected his own face breaking into a grin. 'What are you looking so happy about?'

'The other trials, Alex. That's the answer.'

'What do you mean. Not to run a trial here at all?'

'No, silly. It's much simpler than that.' She was almost dancing. 'I know ours is one of the first centres, but several others are being set up now, at this moment. All we have to do is contact all the other trials and ask for copies of their protocols. Then we can be sure that ours will start from the same basic premises as all the rest!'

Ellen Barker entered the room just then and nearly dropped the tray she was carrying.

'Just minutes ago the two of you looked as if the end of the world had been declared, so come on, what's been going on since I left?'

Rebecca and Alex were both trying to speak at once, the torrent of words becoming impossibly tangled.

'Whoa! One at a time!' Ellen laughed.

'You tell her, Becca. It was your brainwave.' And he reached for a cup of tea and grabbed a handful of biscuits.

'Well, I wouldn't have thought of it if you hadn't said. . .'

'For heaven's sake, will somebody tell me what's going on around here?' Ellen complained. 'Does this mean that we can get down to some real work now?'

While they drank their tea Ellen was brought up to date on the latest development and volunteered to contact the other groups as soon as possible. The three of them were now confident that one major stumbling block had been sidestepped, but deep inside Rebecca knew that this was only a lull in the continuing storm. She and Alex had too many differences of opinion and were each too strong-willed to give ground easily, especially over something which meant so much to them.

Rebecca was also becoming more certain with every clash of wills that there was something fundamental which was preventing Alex from accepting her profession. Not that he had said anything, but she sensed a deep well of anger inside him which spilled out sometimes.

And yet. . .he seemed to be more accepting of what she was telling him, so maybe there was a chance. . .

They had resumed their meeting in good spirits until Alex proposed that all the patients who were already scheduled for surgery should be excluded.

'Certainly not,' Rebecca retorted. 'You've seen for yourself that patients on your lists can benefit from chiropractic care, especially those who can't tolerate the quantities of painkillers they need. Just because they are already on your list, it shouldn't deprive them of any other help,' she defended hotly.

'Well,' Ellen broke in, 'in an ideal world they would all be able to have physiotherapy before as well as after their surgery, but we come up against the usual brick wall—not enough time, space or staff. I would be very glad if some of them were able to see Becca; then I would have a better idea of what is possible.'

'There could be some degree of overlap at some time in the future,' Rebecca proposed eagerly, 'with the best of your efforts joining with the best of mine to produce a package which could be made available to everyone diagnosed as needing replacement surgery. In the meantime, that would only confuse the issue as far as these trials are concerned.'

'But that needn't stop us talking about it.'

'So, now that the two of you have ganged up on me, what exactly are you proposing? That all patients are included in the lottery regardless, and those unlucky to be chosen for either of your two forms of treatment are taken off the list? If that is so, I can tell you there will be an almighty row, and I would be leading it.' Alex was keeping his temper, but only just.

'Certainly not. . .'

'Of course not. . .'

Their sentiment was unanimous and Rebecca continued heatedly, 'What sort of heartless idiots do you take us for? That is the last thing we would expect.'

'In fact,' Ellen chimed in, 'I wouldn't be surprised if the surgical patients who are chosen for either of the other two modes aren't absolutely delighted.'

'Why should they be delighted? They've already seen an orthopaedic surgeon and had all their tests. They know what is wrong and what is going to be done about it. Why would they welcome going all the way through the mill again?'

'It's human nature, Alex,' Ellen answered gently. 'It's proof that someone's thinking about them, doing something for them.'

'Putting them through unnecessary pain for dubious results? I'm sure they'll be delighted.'

'That's what the whole exercise is for, isn't it?' Rebecca's voice was quiet. She was coming to realise just how far there was to travel before she and Alex would have any chance of a relationship.

'Whether you like it or not, Alex, the MRC trial

showed that chiropractic treatment is effective, and subsequent reports have recommended that this treatment should be made available through the NHS. The only thing yet to be decided is *how* it is going to happen.

'I would have thought,' she continued, her personal disappointment colouring her words, 'that a caring physician would reach with both hands for something which will help his patients cope with their disability while they are waiting for surgery, and which also offers the possibility of a faster, more complete recovery.

'Apart from anything else, it could mean appreciable savings in time and money, which will mean that more patients can be seen and waiting lists get shorter.'

There was a profound silence after she finished speaking. Rebecca herself had fixed her gaze on the pencil she held between her two hands, knowing that if she was to look at Alex she would crack.

The sudden snap of the pencil startled them all, and they each watched while Rebecca put the two broken halves neatly together on the pile of files in front of her.

'I need a breath of fresh air,' she said, rising as slowly as one of the patients they had just been discussing. 'I'll be back in a few minutes.'

As she left the room she heard Ellen mutter, 'No, Alex. Let her go.' Before the door closed behind her.

She found herself in a ladies' cloakroom without knowing how she had got there. Bracing her back into a corner, she was glad to feel the coolness of the white tiled walls against the heat of her palms and waited for the horrible feeling of nausea to pass.

Long moments later she was able to take a deep breath. As shakily as a very old woman she made her way to one of the basins and splashed cool water on her face, heedless of what it would do to her appearance.

A quick glimpse in the mirror had told her that she looked terrible, her eyes darkly staring. Lost-looking.

That was exactly how she felt. Lost and alone.

Oh, it was nothing new to feel isolated. Her parents had seen to that. All her life she had felt as if she was not important enough for them to take much interest in her. Her defiance of their wishes as to her choice of career had brought down their wrath, but it had not severed any essential warmth between them because it had never existed in the first place—not that they were uncaring parents. It was more a case that their minds were almost totally occupied with their respective professions.

Since she had met Alex Marshall she had started to wonder if there might perhaps be a chance for the two of them, some possibility that the attraction which she had felt towards him the first time they'd met might grow into something rare and wonderful.

She knew that his opposition to complementary therapy was unusually violent, but she could appreciate that he would feel he had to fight for the welfare of his patients.

It just seemed so impossible at the moment that they would ever have a chance to find something together if he was wilfully throwing obstructions in their way.

Drying her face on a fresh paper towel, she smoothed back the tendrils of coppery hair which had escaped from her ponytail. Not having thought to pick up her bag as she left the conference-room, she was unable to repair her make-up, but, giving herself a stern look in the mirror, she turned and left the room, her head up and her shoulders back.

Alex was the only one in the room when she returned.

'Are you all right?' His voice had the tone common to men when they were out of their depth with displays of emotion. Although she knew it didn't reach her expression, Rebecca was amused by his discomfort.

'Of course.' She was pleased that she sounded so calm and unconcerned in spite of her turbulent feelings. 'Is Ellen coming back, or what?'

A frustrated look crossed his face as she changed the topic of conversation.

'She's just gone ahead to check in with her department before she joins us in the canteen for lunch.'

Rebecca seized her chance eagerly and chattered brightly as they left the conference-room and started along the corridor.

'You mean I'm going to find out if all those horror stories about staff canteens are really true?'

Her animation faded as they found themselves together in an otherwise empty lift.

'Becca, I'm sorry.' He dragged the fingers of both hands through his hair leaving it with its familiar windblown look. 'We need to talk,' he declared firmly. 'Shall I pick you up this evening or would you rather meet me somewhere?'

Her heart thumped heavily for a few beats then settled into its normal rhythm.

'No, Alex.' Her voice was quiet but no less firm. 'I don't think it's a good idea for us to start seeing each other in a social way at this stage of the trials. It's just making everything more difficult. Perhaps later on. . .' She allowed her words to die away, unwilling even now to deny herself some small hope.

'Do you mean that these trials take precedence over everything else?' he demanded.

'Not in the way you mean.' She sounded weary even to her own ears. 'I just mean that this is an extremely stressful time and I can't cope with anything more at the moment.'

He was looking at her, holding her eyes with his and gazing soul-deep for several long seconds before he released her with a sigh.

'All right. I'll agree with that for the moment. But we will be having that talk—soon.' And there was a world of determination in his words.

CHAPTER FIVE

SEVERAL days passed without any contact from Alex and Rebecca found it difficult to decide which emotion was stronger—relief from the turbulence he caused in her feelings or depression that the world seemed a duller place without his presence.

There wasn't even the prospect of another meeting to look forward to; at least, not until the consultation with the other trials groups was complete.

Rebecca was angry with herself that thoughts of Alex seemed to intrude whatever she was doing.

The phone would ring and her heart would sink when it wasn't his voice; she would see a tall, broad-shouldered man ahead of her, but when his dark head turned it was never Alex—and then she was furious with herself that she should even have wished that it were.

She had just shown her next patient through that Friday afternoon when there was a knock at the door.

'Please excuse me, Mr Chapman. At this rate I'll have to get myself a receptionist.'

She opened the door with a friendly smile which disappeared at the shock of her visitor's identity.

'Alex!' Inwardly she cursed the breathless tone of her voice and cleared her throat. 'What can I do for you?'

One dark eyebrow nearly disappeared under the tousled hank of hair which curved forward on to his forehead, and the expression which accompanied it made Rebecca catch her breath.

'Would it be convenient for me to sit in on the last of your patients this afternoon? I've been in meetings all week and haven't been free to come until now.'

Why was his voice so rich, why was his tone so seductive when the words he spoke were so mundane? Rebecca shook her head to clear her thoughts and hastily broke into speech when she saw the dark scowl which crossed his face as he misunderstood her action.

'Yes, of course. I mean. . .if Mr Chapman agrees. . .' Her words faded away as Alex took matters into his own hands and strode into the room to introduce himself.

For some while, Rebecca could not understand why the atmosphere in the treatment-room seemed so frosty. As usual, Alex had explained his presence to Mr Chapman and had taken himself to his customary position. After that, nothing had been the same, but for the life of her Rebecca could not pinpoint why— until she started treating her patient.

About the same age as Alex, Mr Chapman was a keen sportsman who had injured himself during a bout of judo.

'Didn't land a kick properly and messed my knee up good and proper,' he groaned in explanation to Alex as Rebecca probed. 'Then the hospital put me on crutches to keep my weight off my knee and I managed to tie my shoulders and neck in knots.'

'Could you turn face-down for me, Mr Chapman?' Rebecca interrupted his rueful tale to position him for the next stage of his treatment. 'Now, then. I need you to relax completely this time, otherwise we won't be getting very far. No fighting me as you did last time.'

His answering chuckle was almost lost under the sharp query in Alex's voice.

'Fighting you?' Rebecca glanced across the room and

found that, far from leaning comfortably against the wall, he was now standing just a few paces away, every muscle taut with aggression.

'Just a descriptive term.' Rebecca managed to force the words out past the surprise which had gripped her by the throat. 'As you can see, Mr Chapman has very well-developed muscles on his torso and, if he tenses up, not only does it make my job harder, but it can also make the process more painful than necessary for the patient.' As she worked her way through the various muscle groups to check for tenderness, she glanced across at Alex, fully expecting him to have relaxed again. Instead, he seemed to be more tense than ever, his gaze fixed on the motion of her hands on her patient's back.

Puzzled, she looked down, wondering what he was frowning at so fiercely. It was several long seconds as she watched the movement of her slender hands on the powerful, tanned breadth of the muscular body in front of her before the germ of an idea started to grow. She looked at Alex's face as she struggled with the temptation to test her theory, then succumbed.

'Now, I'll just do some mobilisation of your thoracic region,' she murmured, having discarded the idea of practising the massage techniques she had picked up from a fellow student several years ago.

Mr Chapman groaned.

'Am I hurting you?' Rebecca queried, her attention momentarily divided between the two men in the room. Mr Chapman had the more muscular body; after all, he had spend long hours devoted solely to developing those muscles. But it was Alexander Marshall's body— not the look of it, just its presence in the room—which made her own body come alive.

'God, no!' Mr Chapman groaned again. 'You could

do that to me forever. It feels. . .aah!. . . It feels fantastic!'

Rebecca continued to work her way up his back using the heels and sides of her hands to deliver the thrust which would release the muscle spasm.

'Don't you think you've done enough for one session?' Alex's voice was sharp, but there was a husky undertone which she had last heard when they had been. . .

'Dr James.' The husky tone had disappeared from Alex's voice, replaced with a more urgent note which broke into her musing.

'Right, Mr Chapman.' Rebecca concluded. 'I'll see you again next week, but in the meantime get your fiancée to continue with those exercises I showed her last time. Between the two of us, you're progressing well!'

As her patient left the room, Rebecca glanced across at Alex just long enough to note the residual flush across the taut planes of his cheekbones. Then, before he could catch her watching him, she concentrated on making her final notations in her patient's file. She knew that from his position Alex would not be able to see her face so she permitted herself the luxury of a small grin.

He may have been brusque and chilly with her when he arrived, but the sight of her hands on the body of another man had definitely had an effect on him!

Ten minutes later she had dropped the catch on the front door and they were alone in the house.

She was walking swiftly along the corridor which went past the door to her treatment-room on her way to the kitchen when one lean tanned hand flashed out through the doorway to capture her wrist. The momentum carried her round in an arch until she suddenly came to rest against the familiar breadth of a warm male chest.

She gazed up at him, her startled eyes as dark as rich chocolate.

'You did that on purpose, you red-headed witch!' the husky voice accused just before his mouth took possession of hers.

His arms encircled her body, holding her so tightly against him that she could feel the beat of his heart against her—or was it her own heart she could feel beating so fast that it was the only sound left in the universe.

Her hands crept up to his shoulders and her fingers gave in to temptation, twining themselves in the silky profusion of his ruffled hair.

She was surrounded by him, the strength of his arms holding her against the solid power of his body, her eyes tight shut so that her other senses were flooded with stimuli. Her ears became sensitive to the changing pace of his breathing, her nose to the warm musk of his skin and her mouth to the dark sweetness of the tongue which filled it.

Long moments later they drew apart, as breathless as if they had run a marathon.

With a rueful chuckle Alex leant his forehead against hers. 'You did, didn't you?'

'Did what?' Rebecca couldn't remember what they had been talking about—she could hardly remember her own name. 'Oh, that. . .' She stopped just too late.

'Yes, you little witch, *that*. You knew exactly what effect it would have on me.' He slid both hands down her back to her hips and pulled her firmly against himself so that there could be no mistaking his meaning.

Involuntarily Rebecca found herself moving against him, adjusting the contact between them until they were perfectly matched the whole length of their bodies.

'Sorceress,' he hissed, running his fingers through the coppery mass of her hair and releasing it to fall in a gleaming mantle over her shoulders, then slid them slowly down the length of her back to cup around the smooth swells of her buttocks, pulling her tight against his arousal.

'I was determined to obey your wishes, to keep this relationship between us purely professional. But you make it impossible.' He cupped her face between his hands and angled his head to touch his lips to hers.

'Damn.' He released his breath in an explosive burst as the phone on the table beside them jangled its summons. 'You haven't had time to switch the answering machine on yet, have you?'

Dumbly, she shook her head, her thoughts still totally scrambled by their recent passion.

'You'd better answer it, then.' He stepped back from the contact between them and she felt bereft, the chill of his absence doing nothing to still the thrumming of her pulse rate. 'I'll go and put the kettle on.' His fingers slid down the softness of her cheek in a lingering caress before he turned to leave the room.

Five minutes later Rebecca joined Alex on the couch in her living-room.

'Any problem?' he indicated the phone.

'No. No problem. Just booking in another new patient for Monday.'

'Am I allowed to ask how the practice is doing?' His tone was apparently casual, but Rebecca was slowly coming to know the slight differences in the inflection of his voice, and knew the question was deliberate.

'Surprisingly well, actually. I'm rapidly getting to the stage where I'm full for all three days without resorting to evening clinic hours.' There was a touch of justifiable pride in her voice at this evidence of her unaided success.

'Are you keeping your evenings free for your busy social life?' Once again he spoke lightly but with a deeper significance to his words.

'Eventually.'

'What do you mean, eventually?'

'I mean, eventually my evenings will be filled with a busy social life.'

'What's wrong with your social life now?' He sounded slightly puzzled.

'Nothing's wrong with it, except that it's non-existent.' She smiled wryly.

'But you're meeting people all day. . .'

'And I was at college with hundreds, but,' she shook her head while she organised her thoughts. 'While I was at college, it was too important to me that I should succeed at what I'd fought so hard to do. Since I've qualified, I've been totally wrapped up in starting out in practice. It's been especially difficult because I've moved to a new area.'

'Was that deliberate?'

'You don't miss much, do you?' she smiled then nodded briefly. 'I suppose it was, partly. To move outside the area where I was known; outside my parents' sphere of influence. Perhaps I just wanted the challenge. To stand or fall on my own merits.'

'So you haven't really had the time to start making many social contacts?' he queried.

'If you substitute "any" for "many" you'll be closer

to the truth. I hadn't realised how difficult it was going to be to meet people my own age. There are so few places a woman can go on her own. So few places she would *want* to go alone.'

'I suppose you're right about that.' His tone was reflective. 'I hadn't really thought about it before. And you can hardly start making dates with your patients, can you? It would probably involve you in the thorny question of ethics.'

'Apart from the fact that they come to see me because of some sort of physical breakdown. Who wants to make a date with a crock!' she joked.

'Well, as a strictly non-crocked non-patient, may I suggest that you come out with me tomorrow evening?' He held up his hand as she started to interrupt. 'Before you repeat you objections of the other day, may I clarify the situation?' At his raised eyebrow, she nodded for him to continue.

'I've been invited to a party tomorrow evening. I'm obliged to go, so I was intending just to show my face and leave as soon as possible. If you'd like to come with me, it would be an opportunity for you to start getting to know some of the locals and perhaps making some friends. What do you say?'

Five minutes before Alex was due to pick her up Rebecca was regretting the fact that she had given in to the urge to spend the evening with him.

Granted, they were going to a party, but, as he would probably be the only person she knew, to all intents and purposes they would be spending the evening together. That thought was enough to send a squadron of butterflies into aerial manoeuvres somewhere just under her ribs.

She hoped that her choice of a silk tricot dress the

colour of rich cream was suitable. At least she knew
that the colour suited her and the dress fitted her as if
designed specifically for her, the supple silk flowing
gently over her curves, at once hiding them and revealing them in a tantalising way.

Then the bell rang and all her soul-searching was too
late, her heartbeat pounding at the base of her throat
as she picked up her wrap and bag and went to open
the door.

She had seen Alex in evening dress before, but he
took her breath away all over again, the combination
of elegance and blatant virility overwhelming her.

'Ready to go?' He took the wrap from her nerveless
fingers and flicked it gently to rest around her
shoulders.

'Ready.' She heard the huskiness in her voice and
swallowed quickly to clear it. 'How long will it take us
to get there?' As if she really cared whether they went
there at all!

So much for all her stern lectures to herself, and to
Alex, about keeping their association businesslike. Just
one look at him, just one touch of his hand on her
shoulder and she was ready to follow him anywhere.

As she walked towards the car she heard him pull
the door closed with a final-sounding click and she
stiffened her shoulders. She was not some empty-
headed ninny, she lectured herself firmly; she was a
fully-qualified professional woman, and she would
behave like one.

They had been at the party for nearly an hour and
Rebecca was seriously wishing she hadn't agreed to
come.

The whole atmosphere was similar to many of the
events she had attended with her parents, even though

the average age of those present was a generation younger.

From the moment they had arrived, Alex had been welcomed with open arms.

'Alex, my boy. Glad you could make it,' their host had boomed, a broad smile on his florid face. 'You do know that Sophie's back, don't you. She's in the other room.' His eyes had skated over Rebecca as if she wasn't there, until Alex had drawn her forward and introduced her.

'Jolly good, my dear. The more the merrier. Alex, my boy. Get Sophie to introduce her to some of her young men. Can't have a pretty thing like her on her own.'

Just then their host's attention was caught by a new arrival, giving Alex the chance to retrieve Rebecca's arm.

'Quick,' he hissed, 'into the other room before he sees where we're going.'

Alex's unexpected cloak-and-dagger impression startled Rebecca into a fit of hastily smothered giggles.

'Who is he, for heaven's sake?' she queried quietly when they'd found themselves a drink. 'He's behaving like some stage caricature of blue-blooded gentry.'

'That's probably because he married into it rather than being born to it,' Alex's tone was wry. 'The true gentry I've met aren't in the least like that.

'Actually,' he continued, 'He has made several donations to medical charities.'

'I see. A useful man to know.' She grimaced knowingly. 'And who is Sophie? His wife? After that performance it could even be his favourite dog!'

'His daughter, actually.' His eyes were gleaming in answer to hers, 'But knowing him it could just as easily have been the dog.'

'You know her well, then?' Rebecca found herself asking, a little shiver of dread working its way through her.

'I did, once.' The tone of his voice told her that the topic of conversation was unwelcome, but she refused to change subjects, opting rather for silence.

'We were engaged once,' he added, expressionlessly.

If someone had detonated a bomb, Rebecca couldn't have been more shocked. But why shocked? He was an attractive, wealthy man in his mid-thirties with enough charisma and sex appeal for a dozen others. He had not been kept in cold storage waiting for her.

She found herself gazing at him, knowing that her surprise was showing in her face, and hoping that he would not be able to see the inexplicable underlying feeling of hurt.

'Alex, darling.' The throaty purr came from behind Rebecca and she found herself elbowed out of the way by a voluptuous vision in a slither of scarlet, a riot of artfully tousled blonde hair surrounding a stunningly beautiful face. 'You naughty man. Why haven't you been to see me?' and two arms wound their way around his neck as their lips met.

'Oops,' she chuckled as she drew one scarlet painted nail over his mouth. 'It looks as if I've branded you.'

'Hello, Sophie,' Alex took hold of both her wrists and stepped back from her, then removed the lipstick from his mouth with the handkerchief he took from his pocket. 'You haven't met Rebecca yet, have you?' Alex stepped aside to place an arm around Rebecca's shoulder. 'She's recently moved into the area and set herself up in business.'

'Really!' Rebecca found herself the focus of a pair of skilfully enhanced china-blue eyes. 'Not another of those dreadful boutiques, I hope.'

'No. I'm——'

'Oh, good. I really don't know why they're so popular.' Her gaze travelled dismissively over the understated elegance of Rebecca's dress. 'The choice is so much better in Knightsbridge or Chelsea, don't you think so, darling?' She tucked her arm smoothly into Alex's, her smile coquettish, then turned towards Rebecca, forcing Alex to relinquish his hold on her.

'I'm sorry, was it Rachel. . .?'

'Rebecca.' She spoke her name sweetly, knowing that she was only being asked for effect.

'Of course. Well, Becky, you won't mind it I take Alex away for a moment, will you, only he's got a lot of old friends waiting to see him?'

'I'm sure they'd like to be introduced to Becca, too.' Alex's voice came out as a growl as he disentangled himself again.

'No, don't worry about me, Alex.' Rebecca's tone was sweet enough to cause instant cavities, although how she was managing to speak with her teeth grinding together, she didn't know. 'You run along with Sally here and say hello to all her playmates. I'm sure I'll be able to find someone to hold a conversation with.' And she turned smartly on her heel and made her way swiftly across the room and out of the door.

For an hour or more Rebecca concentrated on introducing herself to the other members of the party, avoiding the groups which Alex was part of and refusing to allow herself even to think about him.

In spite of her initial reservations, she found herself enjoying the chance to start a new circle of friends. As was the way of such things, some were more welcoming than others, while at least two of the men were far more friendly than she would have wished.

At odd times she caught sight of Alex across the

room, his dark head taller by several inches than those surrounding him. Several times she heard the distinctive sound of husky laughter which told her that Sophie was still draped possessively over his arm.

After a while, she felt the need for some solitude and was seated quietly in the corner of a settee having momentarily managed to slip away from one particularly persistent young solicitor.

She was nursing a deceptive glass of plain orange juice and a deep inner excitement at the result of her thoughts. She couldn't wait for the end of the evening to come so that she could be alone with Alex. Alone, so that they could talk seriously about the attraction between them. She needed to find out how he really felt about. . .

Suddenly, she found herself surrounded by a cloud of heavy musk perfume as Sophie joined her, as elegantly as ever, on the settee.

'He's told you about us, of course,' she announced confidently.

'Who?' Rebecca managed to keep the tone of the single word as an innocent enquiry.

'Don't be stupid.' The languid assurance slipped a little. 'Alex, of course.'

'Oh. You mean that you were once engaged? Yes, he did mention it.' Rebecca heard the quick intake of breath caused by the apparent nonchalance of her reply and watched the series of expressions which crossed Sophie's face before she could control it.

'Oh, that!' her words were accompanied by a dismissive wave of her hand. 'That was years ago. We were just children, then.' She turned to fix Rebecca with challenging eyes. 'But we're not children any more. That's why he moved to St Augustine's. So that he would be closer. . .' She let the sentence die, knowing that Rebecca could finish it for herself.

Except that Rebecca knew that it wasn't true—well, how could it be, when Alex had invited her to accompany him this evening? It was just Sophie's spiteful ploy to try to upset her.

Or was it? Had she read too much into an innocently friendly invitation?

'He's good, isn't he?' Sophie's voice broke into her thoughts, forcing her to hide her sudden confusion.

'Good as a surgeon?' she rallied, not sure where the conversation had gone in her absence.

'That, too, by all accounts,' Sophie patronised, 'but what I meant was his piano-playing.'

For the first time, Rebecca noticed that the background music had changed, and was now being played live.

'Alex plays the piano?' Her surprise obviously delighted Sophie.

'Didn't he tell you?' She shook her head pityingly. 'He helped to finance his way through medical school by playing the piano in clubs and hotel lounges around London.

'It was so silly, really, putting himself through all that,' she mused, 'when all he had to do was speak to my father and he would have financed him.' She fixed Rebecca with a taunting look. 'Then we would have been able to get married straight away, instead of wasting all these years.' She raised her left hand to display a stunning ring on the marriage finger—a large central diamond surrounded by a starburst of small stones.

She sat back triumphantly leaving her hand on her slender thigh where the ring could catch the light.

No! Sensation poured through her heart like a land-

slide. Not Alex! Not now, when she had only just
realised as she had sat quietly and analysed her jumbled
emotions that she was in love with him; that he was the
one man she would love for the rest of her life.

Self-preservation had caused her to tilt her head
forward, her hair partially hiding the fact that her face
was clammy with shock. She had felt the colour drain
from her cheeks and knew how dark and bruised her
eyes would look.

Rebecca's pain-crazed thoughts scurried round in
circles, their only constant the recognition of a popular
tune she had last heard when she and Alex had shared
their first meal together.

'His taste in music leaves something to be desired,'
she hit out blindly, not realising until her words echoed
hollowly in the room that he had just finished playing.

There was a deathly hush, broken only by the
embarrassed giggle of one of the women nearby as she
moved away from Rebecca.

Suddenly there was a clear path across the room so
that she could see Alex clearly for the first time since
she had walked away. He appeared totally relaxed as
he sat easily on the piano stool, but Rebecca sensed
the steel in him. He was dark and remote across the
polished expanse of the piano and she looked at him as
if he was a stranger. The expression on his face was
cool and impassive and there was a ruthless set to his
jaw that sent a quiver of awareness through her body.

He held her gaze for long, silent seconds before an
expression of disdain finally entered his eyes and he
dismissively returned them to the keyboard.

No one seemed willing to break the awful silence
until at last he began to play again.

Chopin.

Lyrical and utterly faultless and, for the first few bars, played with his coldly cynical gaze fixed on hers.

Unable to wrench her eyes away from him, she was only vaguely aware of Sophie's departure until she reappeared in Rebecca's vision as she persuaded Alex to move across on the stool to make room for her.

The smile he bestowed on her as he complied was the final straw.

Fearful that her emotions would be all too easily read if he should glance her way again, she fled to the nearest bathroom and locked the door, furious with herself. So much for all her heart-searching. So much for her decision to be strong enough to call a halt to the deepening of any relationship between Alex and herself.

What relationship?

She had obviously been deluding herself that he had anything more permanent in mind than an occasional dinner partner—why had Sophie not been available?— with the possibility of a one-night stand if the opportunity arose. But he had seemed so devastatingly sincere in his wish for her company, wailed her poor bruised heart.

Rebecca fixed her reflection with a stern glare.

This was the last time she was going to skulk in a bathroom. The last time she was going to let Alex Marshall affect her emotions in any way.

From now on, if she had anything to say to him, she would meet him squarely. Anything she wanted to ask, she would do so face to face.

Her primary problem was more down-to-earth. Having insulted the man in front of all his friends, she now had two tasks. First, to apologise for her comment, and then to arrange for a means of transport home.

Decisions made, she left her sanctuary to rejoin the

thinning ranks of party guests, determined to put them into effect as soon as possible.

A quick perusal of each room being used for the party left Rebecca with the immediate fear that Alex had left in her absence. Dismay swamped her. She didn't know whether the courage to make her apology would endure until she was next due to see him, and she was certain that he would not be willing to meet her socially before then.

That left her with the problem of arranging transport.

Although one of the men she had met earlier had offered to see her home, she had known even then that not only had he drunk too much to be safe behind the wheel of a car, but that he would not expect to be sent on his way when he dropped her off.

The only solution she could think of was to find her host and hostess and ask for the use of the phone.

The sound of familiar voices from a room further along the corridor took her footsteps that way. The door was partially open although the occupants of the room were not in sight when she tentatively knocked and pushed the door wider.

Although the central chandelier had been turned on, the room appeared dark because the serried ranks of darkly bound books gave the impression of absorbing the light.

Her entry caused the group of people gathered in front of the imposing fireplace to freeze briefly into a tableau.

'I'm sorry to intrude.' Her hesitant words seemed to set them into motion again. 'But could I use the telephone for a moment to call a taxi?'

Her initial glance at the group had left an indelible impression on her mind's eye. Sophie had been leaning against Alex, her pale hands linked behind the golden tan of his neck as she gazed up at him while her parents smiled approvingly on.

'Pardon, my dear?' Sophie's father was the first to react.

'I. . .it's been very kind of you to have me here,' she stumbled, concentrating on keeping her eyes focused on his face, 'but it's time I was leaving, and. . .'

'There's no need for that.' Alex's voice broke in harshly, and Rebecca's eyes swung across to clash almost audibly with the steel of his. 'I'm ready to leave, too, so I'll be taking you home.' His eyes dared her to object.

'Well, then, I'll be waiting by the front door. . .' Her voice tailed off as she turned away, her hands mangling her bag as they clenched convulsively when her ears picked up the sound of his muttered imprecation.

As they reached the car, Rebecca turned to face Alex, determined to apologise for her appalling bad manners.

'Alex, I'm sorry——'

'No! Not a word,' he gritted. 'Don't you say a word or I'll. . .' He shook his head rather than finish.

The atmosphere in the car was electric with tension the whole of the journey. Rebecca had settled herself into her seat as soon as Alex had unlocked the door, not giving him the chance to offer assistance as he had when they started the evening.

From the corner of her eye she could see how rigidly he was holding his shoulders, and the gleam of white at his knuckles as he gripped the wheel was further mute evidence of his hostility.

Inside, Rebecca was crying with the loss of her first and last love. The first man who had meant more to

FREE! THIS CUDDLY TEDDY BEAR!

You'll love this little teddy bear. He's soft and cuddly with an adorable expression that's sure to make you smile.

PLAY THE MILLS & BOON
LUCKY
STARS
GAME!

Scratch away the silver panel. Then look for the matching star sign to see how many gifts you're entitled to!

	WORTH 4 FREE BOOKS, A FREE CUDDLY TEDDY AND FREE MYSTERY GIFT.
	WORTH 4 FREE BOOKS, AND A FREE CUDDLY TEDDY.
	WORTH 4 FREE BOOKS.
	WORTH 2 FREE BOOKS.

YES! Please send me all the free books and gifts to which I am entitled. Please also reserve a Reader Service subscription for me. If I decide to subscribe I shall receive four superb new titles every month for just £7.20 postage and packing free. If I decide not to subscribe I shall contact you within 10 days. The free books and gifts will be mine to keep in any case. I understand that I am under no obligation whatsoever. I may cancel or suspend my subscription at any time simply by contacting you. *I am over 18 years of age.*

12A4D

MS/MRS/MISS/MR _____

ADDRESS _____

_____

_____ POSTCODE _____

◆ **POST THIS CARD TODAY!** ◆

MORE GOOD NEWS FOR SUBSCRIBERS ONLY!

When you join the Mills & Boon Reader Service, you'll also get our free monthly Newsletter; featuring author news, horoscopes, competitions, special subscriber offers and much more!

◄ TEAR OFF AND POST THIS CARD TODAY! ◄

Mills & Boon Reader Service
FREEPOST
P.O. Box 236
Croydon
Surrey
CR9 9EL

NO
STAMP
NEEDED

her than her career, the first whom she had continued to want to see in spite of his denigration of it.

Now that it looked as if he was irretrievably lost, she had to admit to herself that he was the only man she had ever met for whom she would even have considered giving up the career she had fought so hard for.

Huddling closer to the door, she kept her eyes glued out of the side window for long minutes so that she couldn't see him, until a little voice whispered that this would probably be the last time she would have alone with him; the last few moments when she could pretend to herself that their roller-coaster relationship could have a happy ending.

Surreptitiously, she turned her head until she could see his profile: the hair which he tried to tame but which always seemed to end up ruffled; the smooth line of his forehead leading down to the bump on the lean elegance of his nose; the chiselled perfection of his lips and the determined strength in his chin.

Just a few hours ago she had dared to hope that there was a chance that one day she would have the right to gaze at him to her heart's content for the rest of her life. How painful it was to lose a dream when you had only just dared to dream.

With a sudden jolt she realised that they had arrived in front of her house, and she averted her eyes quickly in case he should see the heartsick expression she was sure she must be wearing.

She opened the door as soon as the car came to a halt, but he was still there, ready to escort her to her door in the same frigid silence which had marked the whole journey home.

Part of her wanted nothing so much as to escape behind her front door even though she knew she had an apology to make. But mostly, she wished he would speak; wanted to prolong to the last minute their time together.

Without warning, he took the key she had ready in her hand and thrust it into the lock. The door was swinging wide ready for her entry when he turned her towards him with startling speed, both arms curling about her body with almost vicious strength to pull her against him.

The street-light was blotted out by his head, leaving the expression on his face hidden as he swooped down to cover her mouth with his.

There was an aura of menace about the intensity of his kiss until she parted her lips, her love for him making her helpless to do anything else. Then, as their tongues met in a duel of stunning power, she gave her heart into his keeping forever, knowing, now, that nothing could ever come of it.

CHAPTER SIX

IN SPITE of a largely sleepless night, Rebecca was immaculately dressed and her make-up, although rather heavier then usual to cover the dark circles under her eyes, was perfect.

Mrs Marshall was due for an appointment today and, although it was extremely unlikely that Alex would accompany her, she was determined that his mother would have nothing untoward to tell him about her chiropractor's state of health.

Even though she had told herself that Alex wasn't coming, she couldn't tell her heart not to take a dizzying dive into the pit of her stomach when Phyllis Marshall telephoned to cancel her appointment.

'I'm so sorry to leave it to the last minute like this, my dear, but. . .' She seemed to be trying to choose her words carefully, and Rebecca's spirits sank even lower at the thought that maybe it was at Alex's request that she had cancelled.

'Did you want me to move the appointment later in the week?' she suggested, annoyed with herself for sounding so hopeful.

'I'd love to, my dear, but. . .well. . . There's been a bit of an accident. My dog has. . . Oh, dear, I don't know what to do. I'll have to ring you as soon as. . . Oh, I'm sorry dear. I'll pay for the broken appointment when I come in next time. I must go.'

'Well.' Rebecca exclaimed aloud. 'That was most peculiar,' and she raised her shoulders in a puzzled shrug, rather at a loss to know what to make of it.

At least it seemed as if it was only circumstances which had caused her to cancel, and not the behest of one autocratic son, which was a small enough reason for her to take consolation.

Even though the next few days were busy, with a rise in the number of patients booking in to see her, and several phone calls backwards and forwards between herself and the physiotherapy department and Alex's secretary, there was still an uncanny feeling of emptiness inside her.

The little *frisson* of excitement deep inside which had seemed to have become a permanent resident since she had met Alex Marshall had all but disappeared. Sometimes it was still there when she first woke in the morning, but as soon as she remembered their last disastrous evening together, it soon died.

The only thing she couldn't stop was the heartfelt wish which came over her just as she relinquished control over her thoughts before sleep finally overtook her. Then she had to admit that she longed with all her heart to be granted just one more chance. One last meeting to try to explain. . .to try to persuade. . .but when she awoke, her heart still light with remembered dreams, she had to force herself to be realistic. Such second chances only happened in films or between the pages of books.

It was just over a week before she heard from Phyllis Marshall again, although at first she didn't recognise her voice and wondered if she was recovering from a cold, her voice sounded so strange.

'Is it possible that you could see me either as the last patient this morning, or last thing this afternoon,' came the husky whisper.

'I could make it for five o'clock this afternoon, if that's convenient?'

'Is that your last appointment, my dear? I'm sorry to be such a nuisance but. . .'

'Yes, that's the last one. I'll see you then, shall I?'

At odd moments throughout the day, Rebecca's thoughts went back to that brief conversation, the strange sensation growing that something was not right about it.

Phyllis Marshall had seemed uneasy about something. Had her son tried to forbid her making any further appointments? She had certainly seemed almost. . .furtive in her manner. Still, all would be revealed at five o'clock.

For the first time, Mrs Marshall was late for her appointment and, for a few moments Rebecca wondered whether she should telephone to find out what was happening.

Just then, an unfamiliar car drew up and parked outside the practice. The two occupants appeared locked in discussion for several seconds before both doors opened.

First, Phyllis Marshall stepped out from the driving seat, then the all-too-familiar figure of her son, looking less than eager to come into the practice.

'Don't force yourself!' Rebecca muttered viciously. 'I'm not that desperate to see you—you can stay in the car for all I care!' She stiffened her shoulders briefly before they slumped dejectedly.

Of course she cared! Of course she wanted to see him, no matter how averse he was to her company.

The door opened to admit her two visitors. Rebecca waited for several long seconds hoping that Alex would look at her, but he held himself stiffly aloof gazing straight ahead at her framed certificates.

So, that's the way he felt about her now, was it? Well, two could play at that game.

'Mr Marshall, if you would like to take a seat, I'll just take your mother through to. . .'

'No, my dear. It's not for me.' Two pairs of eyes swung instantaneously towards her.

'Who. . .?'

'What. . .?'

Phyllis Marshall wrung the strap of her handbag nervously. 'Oh, dear. I was afraid it would. . .'

'Mother.' His voice was as icily furious as Rebecca had ever heard it. 'What scheming have you and the good doctor been up to.'

'What——?' For a moment Rebecca was speechless at the implied accusation. 'What do you mean, scheming?'

'Alexander, dear, it isn't her fault. It was all my own idea. I was feeling so guilty because it was my Amber who caused the accident in the first place.'

'Go on.' His expression would have done a judge in a murder trial proud.

'Well, you've been flat on your back for nearly a week dosing yourself with all those pain-killers, and you know what a rotten patient you are, and I remembered talking to that Mr Parnell last time I was here. He was telling me that Dr James was able to make a difference on his very first visit, so——'

'So,' he interrupted her flood of words, 'you took it on yourself to make an appointment for me with Dr James without my knowledge or agreement.' His steely gaze was now fixed on Rebecca's pale face. 'Correct me if I'm wrong, but I would hardly have thought that was ethical?'

'If it was true, I would agree with you.' Rebecca's words were clipped.

'Meaning?'

'Meaning that I knew as little about your mother's intentions as you did.' His snort of disbelief made her temper rise rapidly towards explosion point.

'She's quite right, you know, Alexander. That's what I've been trying to tell you.' Phyllis Marshall's face was woebegone. 'I knew you would never climb down off your high horse, in spite of the fact that you're in pain. I thought if I could just get you here. . .'

'No, Mrs Marshall,' Rebecca interrupted firmly. 'It doesn't work that way. I would never accept him as a patient. . .'

'What? You would refuse to treat me?' He sounded quite outraged.

'Certainly. If a patient does not want to come to me, I will not accept them as a patient. Similarly, if I were to examine you and find that your condition was outside my expertise, I would recommend you to the appropriate discipline.' She paused briefly, holding his steely gaze with the honest power of her own dark brown eyes before she turned to his mother.

'Well, Mrs Marshall, if you don't want to take advantage of this appointment time, I can shut up early for the day.'

There was a long pause while Phyllis Marshall and her son fought a silent battle of wills. Rebecca was fascinated to see the tide of red which crept along Alex's cheekbones before he finally broke eye-contact with his mother to turn to her.

'No. I mean. . . Don't shut up yet. As I'm here, I might as well let you have a look at me.'

'And so gracious, too.' Rebecca muttered as she caught Mrs Marshall's eye. 'Well, then,' she invited, 'if

you would like to go through to a changing cubicle?
Did you want to have your mother come through with
you?' She was following him out of the reception area
and knew he had heard Phyllis Marshall's snort of
laughter when even the back of his neck turned brick-
red.

She shut the door crisply behind them.

The notes Rebecca took at the start of the case
history confirmed the basic information she had already
learned about Alex from his mother and from her own
social meetings with him.

Strangely, she found herself lingering over the form-
filling aspect of the consultation until she realised the
reason—she was nervous of commencing the next
stage, the point where she would actually have to touch
his body.

To cover the fact that her hands were trembling
slightly, she crossed to the basin in the corner and ran
them under the hot water for a moment.

'Right.' She turned, drying her hands as she spoke.
'If you would come over to the mirror, here, and take
off your gown.' She could hear the quiver in her voice,
but her breath disappeared entirely when he slipped
off the thin gown and deposited it on the back of the
chair.

He was magnificent.

Tanned and muscular with broad shoulders tapering
into a lean waist. It was so unfair. Standing behind him
as she was, she could see him in his entirety, the
perfection of his back exposed to her avid gaze with
the simultaneous reflection of his dark hair-dusted
chest. Her eyes drifted down towards the stark black
of his underpants before she could control them.

Rebecca shook her head. How was she supposed to

keep her mind on her job with temptation like this in front of her.

'What's the matter?' He must have seen her shake her head.

'If you would like to look straight ahead, you will notice that you are carrying your right shoulder about an inch lower than your left. . . No! Don't try to correct it at this stage. Just relax your shoulders.

'Now,' she continued briskly, getting into her stride, 'if you would step forward on to the scales in front of you. They are a matched pair, and I want you to put one foot on each and then look straight ahead again.'

'Why? What will that tell you?' he queried as he followed her directions.

'It's a useful diagnostic aid in that it can show up minor imbalances—as in your case.'

'What do you mean? I'm standing with my weight evenly over both feet.'

'That's how it feels to you, is it?' She knew he would be able to hear the smile in her voice, and it grew as he looked rapidly down at the scales.

'There are two stones' difference between the weight on either scale. How did you do that?' His tone was rather belligerent, but Rebecca had expected it, having come across that reaction before.

'If you think I have pre-set the scales, you can turn round so that your feet change positions, but I promise that the readings will be the same.

'You hurt your back when your mother's dog tangled you in the lead and pulled you over, and as a result of the protective muscle spasm in your back, it has changed your weight distribution.'

While she was speaking, Alex had taken the opportunity to turn around and test the scales again and Rebecca nearly groaned aloud. He was too close, and her hands were itching to touch him in a far from clinical way.

She collected her wayward thoughts rapidly, before he could see the effect he was having on her concentration.

'I'm now going to do a range of tests on you. Some orthopaedic ones you'll recognise, but some are chiro-practic tests.'

She stood behind him and placed one hand firmly on his shoulder and pressed down firmly, bending his body to the side, then repeated the test on the other side.

'Kemp's manoeuvre is positive on the right,' she commented as she noted her findings, then tested his range of motion in flexion and rotation.

'You can't flex to the right, and your rotation is restricted. Now, can you lie on your back on the couch so that I can test your reflexes?'

She stood close by while he lowered himself gingerly on to the couch, but he managed without assistance.

'You'll be pleased to hear that your reflexes are fine, which indicates that there is no nerve-root irritation.' She had been aware of his eyes following her every move and was glad it was time for him to turn over for the next set of tests.

'Nachlas is positive on the right,' she confirmed as she pressed on his sacrum and lifted his thigh. 'As the other tests were negative, it would indicate a simple sacroiliac strain.' She lowered his thigh to the couch and slid her hand out from the warm hair-sprinkled weight, surprised when her hand seemed to tingle long after the contact was broken.

'When did you last have any X-rays taken? Were any done at the hospital?'

He rolled over slightly so that he was facing her once more.

'No, I haven't had any taken since I broke my arm as a child.' At her raised eyebrow he flashed her a sudden grin. 'I fell out of a tree!'

The unexpected grin was enough to double her pulse-rate. It was so unfair. If she had to fall in love at all, why did it have to be with some one who was already engaged?

Working in the subdued light of the X-ray room gave her time to order her thoughts, especially when he started questioning her again.

'I would have had these X-rays taken with the patient lying down. It would give a clearer view.' He should have felt at a disadvantage standing there with his legs naked up to nearly mid-thigh, but his censorious tone belied that fact.

'So would I, if I were only taking them to rule out the possibility of breaks or disease.' Rebecca paused while she slid the cassette containing the film into the bucky and locked it into position. 'But as I'm more interested in the function of the spine as a whole, it makes more sense to take them load-bearing.'

The two plates were quickly taken and they returned to the treatment-room.

'Now. Just a few helpful hints—although you shouldn't need reminding!' How painful it was to joke light-heartedly with him, as if he were no more than a casual friend.

'No hot water-bottle, no matter how comforting it feels. You'd do better to put a packet of frozen peas on the area for a couple of minutes at a time. Similarly, no sitting in a hot bath. You'd better stick to showers for a while.

'You'll find it easier to stand or lie down, but it will help if you can take some short brisk walks. No dawdling, no jogging and no sitting in long-winded meetings!'

'Some situations mean I have to sit—I can hardly walk up and down while I eat.' The objection had a weary tone which tugged at Rebecca's heartstrings.

'In the absence of someone to minister to your every need, you will have to find a couple of blocks of wood or two house bricks to prop under the back legs of your chair. With the seat tilted forward it will take some of the strain off your lower back.'

She paused and raised one tawny eyebrow at him. 'Any other questions? If not, I'll just see if I can give you a little relief before you get dressed. Then I'll get straight on with developing your plates so you can see them next time.'

'Aren't you going to treat me properly now?' He sounded appalled. 'Why can't you. . .?'

'I know you're in pain, but just think as a physician for a moment,' she interrupted sternly. 'I know what you've done to yourself, but until I see the pictures I won't know why it happened; the predisposing factors. Until then I don't want to do anything that could make it worse.'

'I'm sorry. Of course, you're right. It's just so. . .'

'. . .difficult having to be on the receiving end for a change?' Rebecca completed the sentence for him, and he nodded wearily.

Rebecca positioned him on his side and gently stretched the region of his left sacroiliac, then helped him to his feet.

'As I said, get some ice on it, and you should start to feel a bit easier.'

She watched wistfully as Alex left the room, his gait long and smooth in spite of his pain. She shook her head and went out to join Phyllis Marshall.

'You can have him back in a minute,' she smiled and watched the worried expression lift from his mother's face.

'Is he going to be all right? How soon will he start to feel better?' She hadn't entirely conquered her fear.

'As I told you when you first came here, each person is unique. Obviously, I'll do my best to get him better as soon as possible. . .' she heard the slight noise behind her which signalled his arrival '. . .for your sake as much as his, as he's such a terrible patient!' Her quip was rewarded by Mrs Marshall's peal of laughter at her son's expense, and Rebecca turned in time to catch Alex's wry self-mocking grin.

A sudden thought occurred to her—an impulse too tempting to miss.

'Have you any meetings booked for tomorrow morning?'

'I don't think so,' his expression was slightly wary. 'Why? Is there a meeting planned at the hospital that I haven't been informed about?'

'No. It's not that. It's just. . .I thought you might want to come in first thing to see your X-rays and get started on the treatment proper.' She held her breath, not certain whether she wanted him to accept or refuse.

'What time?' he queried, then, 'I didn't think you opened for patients tomorrow.'

'Well, no, not usually, but. . .' What could she say? Not the truth—that she was willing to take any chance of spending time with him. Perhaps. . .'Won't it make it easier for you not to be seen as a patient of mine by the other patients you've met?'

There was a long pause while he held her gaze, dark brown skewered by steely grey, his face stony.

'I'll be here at nine-thirty, if that suits you?' His deep voice was coldly polite. At her silently nodded agreement he ushered his mother out of the door then halted at the threshold to fire a parting salvo.

'I didn't realise you thought me so petty as to need

to hide behind my professional status like that. I'm just a man, Becca, with the same collection of bones and muscles as everyone else.' He closed the door silently.

Not exactly the same as everyone else, Rebecca thought. His were the only bones and muscles which made hers grow weak with wanting. . .wanting what she couldn't have.

Although Alex was going to be her only patient that morning, Rebecca was determined to behave totally professionally.

It didn't matter that her nerves were so on edge that she was nearly jumping out of her skin; that her hands shook with a fine tremor. She stood in front of the full-length mirror to check her appearance yet again. Yes, she still looked as neat as the last time she had looked; as neat as she always looked when she was ready to greet a patient.

The only difference was the shine in the eyes and the touch of vulnerability to her softly coloured mouth.

The doorbell nearly sent her into orbit, her heart beating frantically to catch up with the sudden surge of adrenalin.

She clenched her fists and walked steadily through to open the door.

A stranger stood there.

Oh, it was Alex Marshall, but as she had never seen him before. This man was dishevelled and unshaven, his cheeks pale and his eyes red-rimmed and sunken.

'Alex!' Her hand went out to assist him into the room, and her heart went out to him in his obvious pain.

'What happened? Have you had another accident?' She knew her love must be clear in the tone of her voice; she was powerless to prevent it. Luckily for her, he was in no fit state to realise it.

'No accident,' he growled, 'just me, being a pig-headed bloody fool.' His self-disgust was evident.

'Didn't you use the ice?' Rebecca questioned as she ushered him straight through to the treatment-room.

'Oh, yes, I used the ice. And I walked, and I didn't sit in a hot bath, nor use a hot water-bottle. . .' He paused involuntarily as he drew in a sharp breath as a result of trying to manoeuvre himself out of his shirt.

'But, if you——'

'I did everything you told me to. . .' He sounded outraged, and in her state of sensitivity Rebecca was sure that it was all directed at her advice.

'But——' she tried again, and again he interrupted to continue.

'I did everything, and when I got up this morning, I felt so much better that I decided to drive myself here.' He paused again to catch his breath. 'Then I dropped the keys and, without thinking, I bent down to pick them up—without bending my knees.

'By that time Mother had left to go shopping and there wasn't time to get a taxi, so. . .'

'You drove yourself here.' Rebecca completed the unfinished sentence. 'You're an *idiot*. All you had to do was phone to let me know you would be a little late.' She sighed heavily. 'Let's see what you've done to yourself.' And she positioned him as comfortably as possible on the treatment couch. 'I'll show you your pictures when you can stay upright long enough to focus on them.'

Gently, she palpated the whole length of his spine pausing at intervals to note her findings, then continued with an abbreviated version of the examination she had conducted the previous day.

'Well, you don't seem to have done yourself any further damage, although your pain level is markedly higher.'

'You're telling me!' he muttered sarcastically into the head-piece of the couch, then added, quickly, 'I'm sorry, I don't mean to take it out on you when I know it's all my own fault.'

'It's so easily done,' Rebecca soothed. 'Especially when you had started to feel so much better. It's harder to remember to take it gently.'

Alex tried to twist his body to look at her and yelped at the sudden stab of pain.

'Lie still and relax while I see if I can free things up a bit.' Rebecca switched herself off from outside stimuli and concentrated on visualising the structures beneath the skin. Several times she repositioned him to treat him in a series of moves which brought forth a cacophony of clicks and cracks.

Finally, she palpated the length of his spine again, right from the top at the base of his skull down to, and including his sacroiliac joints. She was pleased to note the marked easing of several areas of tension, and ran her hands easily over the smooth musculature of his back.

'How does that feel now?' she murmured abstractedly as her hands continued their movement up and down.

'It was fine. . .' he stopped, and Rebecca could feel tension returning along the length of his spine.

'Was?' she questioned, keeping her hands spread over him. 'What's the matter now?'

He groaned and drew in an audible breath. 'Becca, take your hands off my back.'

Rebecca removed them as suddenly as if his back had burst into flames.

'I'm so sorry. Was I hurting you? I don't know. . .'

'No. Yes. Ohhh, Beccca!' As she watched, he rolled his head to the side, this time without a grimace of pain, and she saw the deepened colour along his cheekbones. 'If I were able to turn over, you could see the problem yourself.'

Rebecca's frown of puzzlement gave way to a fiery flush as comprehension dawned.

'Oh! You mean you're. . . I made you. . .' she stumbled to a halt realising that she was only making matters worse.

'Yes,' he mocked gently. 'I was fine all the time you were treating me, but when you started running your hands over my back. . .' His eyes skimmed over the front of her white coat, pausing over the sensitive region where her nipples had tightened in their own blatant reaction. Rebecca glanced down at them herself, supremely aware of their naked shape under her clothes.

'Damn,' he muttered under his breath, 'If I don't start thinking about something else, I'm going to become a permanent fixture on this couch.' He dropped his head back down and mumbled into the upholstery, 'Do you think there's any chance I could beg a cup of coffee?'

'Are you sure you want me to leave you alone just yet?' Rebecca hovered uncertainly beside him, embarrassment warring with her concern for him.

'I think that will be the only cure for what ails me now,' he chuckled hoarsely, and she left, quickly.

Out in the kitchen she was that much further away from the strange sensations which always afflicted her when she was in his vicinity.

Common sense began to reassert itself, and she remembered that the patient in the other room who had just admitted to being aroused by her was engaged to another woman.

By the time the coffee was made, Alex had joined her in he kitchen.

He was still unshaven, but his face looked far closer to its normal colour. His hair and clothes were as neat as a hastily wielded comb and attention to details such as the correct sequence of buttons and buttonholes could make them.

'I'm sorry about that.' He gestured towards the other room. 'I don't usually. . .'

'Please, don't worry about it,' Rebecca dismissed guiltily, knowing that her thoughts had been wandering at the end of the session. Knowing, in her heart of hearts, that she had been stroking him rather than. . .

'Becca?' Why did her name sound like a caress when he said it like that? 'Will you come out for a drink with me this evening?'

'Why?' It was the first word which came to her stumbling brain.

'We need to talk. There are things I should tell you. Things which explain why I've been so. . .' He searched for a word while Rebecca's heart and brain warred frantically.

How she wanted the chance to spend another evening with him, but in this case it would probably be the last. He would tell her about Sophie, and the memory of it would taint all the happy memories so far.

'No!' She spoke more abruptly than she had intended, knowing that if she allowed him time to speak further, he could easily persuade her.

'Just like that?' Was that a glimpse of pain she saw when she fixed her gaze determinedly on him. 'Am I allowed to ask why?'

Out of the blue, the answer came to her.

'You're my patient.'

'So?' he snapped. 'We were colleagues before I became your patient.'

'You said yourself that dating patients becomes a matter of professional ethics. At this stage in my career I can't afford to have anyone pointing a finger at me. Anyway. . .' I can't bear the thought of going out with you while you tell me about Sophie. She had managed to stop herself blurting the words out, but not quite soon enough.

'Anyway what?' His jaw was set in stubborn lines. 'I'm not going until I've had an answer, so you might as well tell me.' His eyes fixed on hers mercilessly.

'Sophie.' The name came out in an unwilling hiss.

'What about Sophie? What has she got to do with this?'

'Well, you're engaged to her, and I don't poach on other women's——'

'What!' he roared. 'Who told you that nonsense?' His hands were gripping her shoulders and he shook her once, starting a gradual avalanche of her once tidy hair.

'N-nonsense?' she stammered. 'B-but she told me herself. She showed me the ring. . .'

'She might have showed you a ring, but it certainly wasn't mine,' he denied vigorously. 'I made the mistake of getting engaged to her once, but I'm not fool enough to do it twice.' He shuddered graphically. 'Do you know what she wanted me to do?' he demanded fiercely, not waiting for a reply before he continued. 'She wanted me to open a fashionable practice in Harley Street, financed by doting Daddy. She couldn't see the difference between reshaping noses and cheekbones and the type of work I do. "It's all bones, isn't it?"' he mimicked Sophie's voice viciously.

The wicked accuracy made Rebecca burst out laughing. Alex joined in briefly, then stopped, his eyes fixed on her face.

'Your face comes alive when you laugh.' His tone was husky and he lifted one lean finger to stroke the tumble of copper away from her cheek, leaving a streak of fire in the wake of his touch.

'Becca. . .if I stop coming for treatment, discharge myself as a patient, will you come out with me?'

'No, Alex. I couldn't.'

'Why not? Now you know there's nothing between Sophie and me. . .'

'I'd feel guilty.'

'Guilty? Why?'

'Because you would be denying yourself the treatment you need just to go out with me,' she said simply.

'But that's crazy.' He raised one hand. 'OK, I can see your logic, but it doesn't make it any easier to. . .'

'Alex,' she interrupted swiftly. 'There is a simple solution. I could refer you to one of my colleagues. I would pass on the X-rays and my findings and they could continue——'

'No!' he erupted. 'I'm not getting on the merry-go-round.'

'I beg your pardon?' Rebecca couldn't believe what she had just heard. Her voice rose a little with each word as the realisation dawned. 'What an utter fool I've been!' she berated herself. 'I actually thought you had opened your hermetically sealed mind. I thought that you were listening when I explained what I was doing and why.'

'I was listening,' he counter-attacked. 'Why do you think I came in to observe?'

'You tell me. It certainly wasn't because you had accepted the principle of my profession. Why was it?

Did you see me as some sort of conquest? My father would have loved it if you had managed to "convert" me, after all his failed efforts.

'Or was it something far simpler?' she mused savagely. 'Was it lust that attracted you? Did I seem like easy prey once you found out how isolated I am here—physically and emotionally?'

She felt the pressure of tears building up behind her eyes and knew for the sake of her own pride that she must not let him see her break.

'Shut the door on your way out,' she instructed as she walked across the room, her shoulders held so stiffly she felt they might crack. 'If you want to continue treatment you are free to make another appointment or ask for your file to be transferred elsewhere.

She nearly made it to the door before he spoke.

'Becca?'

'My name is Dr James.' She knew she sounded choked but didn't dare clear her throat for fear that the torrent would start.

'Don't be pathetic. We've still got to work together on this trials thing.' He spoke harshly.

'Very well, then. Rebecca,' she conceded. 'I'm still Becca only to my friends.'

CHAPTER SEVEN

FROM her refuge in her bedroom, Rebecca heard the front door slam and the later echo of Alex's car door. Then there was silence for such a long time that her conscience pricked her and she went across to the window to see why he had not driven away. Was he in too much pain to drive?

Her vantage point at the window gave her a clear view of the figure sitting in the driver's seat. She couldn't see his head, so his expression was a mystery, but both hands were visible, clenched tightly around the steering wheel.

She watched him, as though coming to a sudden decision, turn the key in the ignition, and heard the purr of the powerful motor. He paused a few seconds longer and then, almost silently, she watched his tail-lights receding until they disappeared around the corner.

That was when her control broke, and she threw herself face downward on her bed to sob out her misery in a storm of grief.

It was so unfair.

For days now she had nursed the despair of believing that he was engaged to Sophie.

Then, when that obstacle was demolished, an insur-mountable one had been uncovered in its place.

In the space of an hour her hopes had been lifted up to the heights merely to be dashed on the rocks. The only consolation she could take was the fact that she had not been tempted to compromise her principles.

Her career was the reason why there was no prospect of a relationship with Alex. Now she would have to put all her energies into that career to make sure that her sacrifice was worthwhile.

Her new decisiveness carried her over the next few days.

She heard nothing from Alex—well, she hadn't really expected to—but no amount of frantic activity could make up for the empty feeling inside.

The next meeting at the hospital in connection with the trials protocol was postponed. The secretary who contacted her cited staff ill-health without specifying which staff member or what illness.

But Rebecca knew, and her heart bled a little knowing that she could have helped to ease his pain and speed his recovery.

After the longest week in her life the phone rang with what seemed at first to be a message of hope.

'My dear, Alexander has asked me to make an appointment for him.'

'He has?' Rebecca was ashamed how breathless her voice was.

'Yes, this time it really *is* for him.' She heard Mrs Marshall's rueful chuckle. 'I learnt my lesson last time, thank you. Anyway, he said he didn't have a chance to see his X-rays last time so he wanted to book the first convenient time on Wednesday.

'I must say, I'll be eternally grateful when you get him sorted out. He's been like a bear with a sore head this last week—or a sore back! Never mind, you do your best for him so he'll return to his usual sunny self.'

Rebecca's mind was off on a track of its own as she

confirmed the appointment time and said her goodbyes.

Sunny nature be blowed! she thought. He'd shown precious little of it to her in the weeks since they'd met. But since that was so, why should her heart have lifted at the prospect of seeing him again? The miserable man only wanted to have a look at his pictures.

It was several hours later that a sudden thought stopped her in her tracks.

If his only interest was in seeing his X-rays, he could have saved himself a visit by putting in an official request from one medical professional to another for the loan of the plates.

Why hadn't he?

Was it because he was using the X-rays as an excuse to see her again?

Warning herself against getting her hopes up, she made herself a few rules. This time she would not allow her common sense to be overruled by the electric current which sizzled between the two of them. This time she would take a mental step backwards and keep a guard on her emotions.

She knew that he was attracted to her and, now, that he was free to follow that attraction. This time she was determined to find out what had built the wall in his mind against her career.

This time she would not allow him to sidestep the issue by hiding his feelings under the camouflage of anger.

'Alex.' Rebecca's greeting was subdued, in contrast to her pulse-rate, which was tumultuous.

'Bec. . . Rebecca,' he returned the courtesy, a brief wince accompanying his rapid correction.

'Did you just want to see the X-rays, or did you want to. . .?'

'No, I came for treatment too, if you're willing to continue. . .'

They were both being so painfully polite that it made Rebecca want to cry.

'That's fine. If you'd like to come through to change.' She led the way through and gave him a clean gown.

'It must cause you a lot of extra work to give each patient a clean gown.' His comment was one she had heard several times.

'They're polycotton and dry easily overnight, but I feel it's important for the patients to have a fresh gown each. Apart from the cleanliness aspect, it helps to make them feel that they're all equally important.'

The conversational trivia helped to smooth over the moments before Alex joined her in the treatment-room, Rebecca finding that her pulse-rate and breathing had returned to normal.

Until he appeared in the doorway, when she found herself fighting for breath again, her heart beating frantically at the base of her throat and filling her ears with thunder.

The breadth of his tanned chest was revealed in the crossover of the front of the gown, the self-coloured belt holding the fabric closely around his lean waist, displaying the sinewed length of his long hair-sprinkeld legs to perfection.

Concentrate, Rebecca admonished herself, silently deciding that her energies would be far better spent trying to find out exactly why Alex was so intolerant of alternative and complementary therapies.

'Have you ever had physiotherapy?' she queried as she preceded him to the X-ray view box.

'No,' he muttered gruffly. 'Never needed it.'

'I know you said you'd generally been very healthy, but I wondered whether you'd had any childhood mishaps. . .?'

'Not that I can remember.' His tone was preoccupied as his eyes fixed on the plates clipped into position. 'Hmm.' The sound was probably uttered subconsciously, but it made Rebecca's lips twitch into a smile.

'You do that very well, you know.'

'Do what?' his glance swung round to encounter her amusement.

'That "hmm" sound you just made. I think there must be special classes to teach all the shades of meaning you can get into it.'

Before he could control it, his own lips curved into an answering smile.

'You're probably right. I don't know where medicine would be without a few "hmm"s.' He held her gaze a few seconds longer before returning to his study of the X-rays.

'Nothing much to see on these,' he pronounced with just a hint of relief in his voice.

'No, they're not bad, on the whole,' Rebecca agreed.

'What do you mean, "on the whole"?' There was an angry defensiveness now.

'Just what I said,' she confirmed calmly. 'Your musculo-skeletal system is in reasonable condition for your age and the type of work you do. There are no serious anomalies or abnormalities. . .'

'Serious? What do you mean? he stepped forward and peered more closely at the films.

'I think we're talking at cross-purposes here.' She made her voice calm. '*You* are looking for gross features, while *I* am talking about functional abnormality.'

'Such as?' he challenged and stepped back.

'Such as. . .the fact that you apparently have one leg nearly half an inch shorter than the other.'

'What!' This time his gaze was focused on the suspect area. 'Hmm,' he murmured absently and, hearing the sound he had made, was forced to chuckle. 'Right,' he said. 'Now, supposing you tell me why you see that as particularly significant. It's hardly something you can do anything about.'

'No, of course not,' she agreed. 'At your age, we can take it that you have stopped growing any taller. . .' She paused as she saw the frown settle on his face, and raised a questioning eyebrow.

'I wish you wouldn't keep saying that. You'll give me a complex.'

'What?' She was lost. 'What did I say?'

'At your age,' he growled. 'You've said it twice now, and I'm beginning to feel positively geriatric.'

'I'm sorry,' she smiled, 'but when you get to. . .' She leant forward to decipher the date of birth printed in the corner of the X-ray as he reached a hand forward to cover the revealing figures and they collided, his hand brushing across the softness of her breast.

They both stopped moving as if frozen in position. The deep tan of his hand was outlined starkly against the pristine white of the jacket which covered the increasing sensitivity of her breast.

As if mesmerised, two sets of eyes, one deep brown, the other quicksilver grey, were fixed on the stark contrast until, with a convulsive shudder, Alex whipped his hand away just as Rebecca was forced to draw breath.

Several seconds passed before either could gather their thoughts, then Rebecca spoke.

'As I was s-saying,' she stumbled, her words as unsteady as her pulse, 'the difference in the leg length is fairly unimportant and affects a large number of the population to a greater or lesser degree. It only really becomes significant when the patient's occupation comes into the picture.'

'I think I see where you're heading, but spell it out for me.' Why did his voice seem so calm? Hadn't he been affected by that little incident?

'You will be the first to admit that you sometimes have to stand in one spot for hours at a time?' Her tone made it a question and he nodded.

'I've sometimes thought that the conditions in an operating theatre are very similar to those on a factory assembly line.' His expression was wry.

'Exactly,' Rebecca agreed. 'And if you were standing on a sloping floor, it would cause uneven stresses in your body all the way up from the floor to your head.'

'Only, in my case, it's me that's crooked, rather than the floor.' He was thoughtful. 'I wonder. . .'

'What?'

'That would probably account for the fact when I'm standing, as I am now——' he gestured down at himself '—I usually stand on one leg and bend the other knee.'

'Exactly. It's the body's way of trying to relieve the stress. It usually copes well enough that you don't even notice you've got a problem until something upsets the system.'

'Like Mother's dog!' he supplied. 'But how do you go about sorting that out?'

'Sometimes, it's enough just to release the protective spasm, and the body then takes up its own form of equilibrium. Sometimes, the overload to the system keeps tripping your fuses, and you need to put a small heel-lift inside your shoe to——'

'A heel-lift!' He sounded horrified. 'Good God, aren't I tall enough?'

Her eyes couldn't resist the invitation to a lightning-fast trip along his magnificent body.

'It's not to make you taller. It's just to lift the short leg slightly to give the taller one a rest.'

He considered the proposition then agreed, grudgingly.

'I suppose it's worth trying, but that's more of a long-term thing. What are you going to do to me today?'

'If you'll come over to the couch and slip the gown off. Make yourself comfortable, face down. . .'

She stepped aside so that she would not be tempted to allow him to brush against her as he passed. Now was not the time for a brain scrambled by lascivious thoughts. It was going to be hard enough to put her hands on him again to start his treatment, without the electrical charge which seemed to pass between them whenever they touched.

'Your erector spinae muscles are well-developed,' she commented as she palpated the long muscular ridges either side of his spine. 'Unfortunately, your height is another disadvantage. It means that you tend to hunch forward as you work, and this can cause stress between your scapulae as well as your low back.'

His skin was tanned and smooth under her touch, and warm, so very warm.

'Take a deep breath——' her voice came out slightly husky and she cleared her throat '—now let it all out. Right out. . . And. . . Good!'

'Ouch!'

'Did I hurt you?'

'Well, no. You startled me. Anyway, something that makes that much noise seems as if it ought to hurt!'

Rebecca found herself laughing at the tone of his voice.

'If you'll turn on to your side now, facing me. . .'

She put a hand out to steady him as he grunted at the manoeuvre, discovering the pleasure of feeling the different textures of the firm skin over his hip where it disappeared into the soft cotton of his brief navy underwear.

'Right, then. Can you straighten out your lower leg while I bend the other knee and. . .' The dark curly hairs on the taut muscles of his calf tickled the palm of her hand as she positioned his bent knee between her thighs.

Immediately, she felt him tense.

'Try to relax,' she coaxed. 'I'm not hurting you, am I?'

Unlike his previous position, she was not facing the back of his head. This time when she glanced up she found his eyes fixed on her face, his expression taut.

'Not exactly. . .' He grimaced.

'Well, then?'

'It's. . . You're. . . Do you have to put my knee there?' the words finally burst out.

Since she had qualified, Rebecca had used this manoeuvre many times without a qualm. This time she fought the fiery blush which rushed over her cheeks, and lost.

'Yes.' Her voice was little more than a whisper as the intimate position of their bodies struck her. This was stupid. It had never bothered her before. But, a little voice inside her head prompted, you've never treated a man you want to. . .

'Yes,' she repeated in a stronger tone. 'I have to position you this way to create the tension I need just here. . .' She leaned forward over him, one hand braced on his shoulder, the other positioned precisely on his back to apply the necessary pressure.

'Tension!' she heard him mutter under his breath, as he finally complied with her request to relax.

Concentrating firmly on the co-ordination betwen the various elements, she successfully completed the lumbar roll.

'That's good. Now, if you'll sit up. . .'

'That's what I tried to do this morning!'

He grimaced in anticipation, the expression changing rapidly as she steadied him again. 'Hey! That's a lot easier to do than it was earlier.' A frown crept over his face. 'It's not going to go straight back to what it was as soon as I get home, is it?'

'It shouldn't. Not unless you do something silly.'

'Don't worry, I won't. I'm staying well away from that dratted dog. One bout of this pain is more than enough!'

'Are you feeling any easier?' Rebecca asked confidently, knowing just from the way he was moving that he felt better.

'Yes. I suppose I am, a bit,' he said rather grudgingly.

'Are you ready, yet, to admit that chiropractic has its place in the scheme of things?' It was meant as a light-hearted joke.

'Hardly.' His reply was crisp. 'There's a lot more involved in it than the relief of a simple back strain.'

Rebecca felt as if he had slapped her face.

'So simple,' she fired back, 'that you have spent the past week in misery while your own profession scrambled about in the dark for a remedy!'

'Well, that's because——'

'It's because,' she interrupted, 'you're too stiff-necked to admit that you *don't* know it all; you *don't* have all the answers.'

'Are you claiming that you do?' he cut back. 'Can you guarantee that you will solve everyone's problems?'

'Of course not,' she scoffed. '*I'm* no megalomaniac.'
Her emphasis made the implication. 'I admit that my
profession has its limitations, but I also know its
strengths.'

'Are you implying. . .?' he broke in hotly.

'I'm implying nothing,' she stated firmly. 'I deal with
damage limitation, damage control. You deal with
crisis situations.'

'Explain what you mean,' he demanded.

'You see patients when they've been in accidents or
when all else has failed. Correct?'

'Well, in a broad sense, I suppose. . .'

'Whereas I, or rather we, hopefully see patients
before they reach that stage. And if we're lucky, we
can put off the evil day when they need to come into
your hands.'

'But, what about those patients, who come to you
when it's already too late? They're just wasting their
time and money. . .'

'No, they're not!' she refuted hotly. 'In fact we've
found that it actually helps to speed things up for
them.'

'How? If they're waiting to find out the results of a
course of treatment. . .'

'I knew you were wary about complementary therapies,' she attacked, 'but I didn't realise just how
blinkered you are! Do you honestly believe that I
would put someone through a course of treatment,
knowing that it was not going to do them any good—
knowing that I was delaying the moment when they
would start the treatment they really need?'

'Some do.' There was a wealth of bitterness in his
voice, but the closed expression on his face told her
that he would not be willing to explain.

'Do you think I'm like that?' she demanded. 'Do you

think my treatment is just wasting your time before you get to the real thing?'

'Well, I won't know how successful your treatment has been until some time has passed, will I?'

'So, in effect you're telling me that you're expecting my treatment to fail. That I'm practising some sort of confidence trick on you?'

'I didn't say that!'

'No, but it's pretty clear that you meant it!' She felt like screaming her exasperation, and took a deep breath. 'Do you admit that your own speciality wasn't able to do anything to help you?'

'The painkillers and muscle relaxants were able to. . .'

'Tablets!' she scoffed. 'Tell me, if the oil-warning light went on in your BMW would you cure the problem by removing the light bulb?'

'What? Of course not! What has that got to do with anything?'

'Pain is a warning light in your body. It's telling you that something is wrong. You don't cure the problem by removing the pain; you must investigate and then remove the cause of the pain. Painkillers only take away the symptoms, they don't remove the cause.' She shook her head sadly, her eyes fixed on his closed expression.

'I don't know why I'm wasting my time talking to such a closed mind.' She took her courage in both hands and asked the question burning in her mind. 'Won't you tell me what happened?'

'Happened?' he queried. 'What? When?'

'Whatever it was that made you switch off.'

'What do you mean, switch off?'

Rebecca realised he was trying to sidetrack her and started her own diversion.

'Tell me, are you still using only the techniques you were taught when you were first qualified, or have you kept abreast of new developments, experimented a bit yourself, perhaps?'

'Of course, I've kept up to date. It's essential. We have to know all the new techniques in case we can use them to help. . .' His voice tailed off as he realised the trap she had set.

'Precisely.' The triumph was tinged with sadness. 'Your mind is open to new ideas and changing methods, but it has a blind spot. It's just my bad luck that I happen to be standing in your blind spot.' She smiled wryly.

'If you'd like to get dressed now, I'll finish making a note of the treatment I've given you.' She sat at her desk, turning her back on the temptation to follow him with her eyes as she heard him leave the room.

Several minutes later Alex joined her in the reception area.

'What do you want to do about making another appointment?' Rebecca had rehearsed the question so that the words would flow smoothly. She didn't know how he would reply, but she was certain deep inside that this would be his last visit.

'I won't make another appointment now.' His words only confirmed her fears, until he continued, 'I'll have to get to the big diary on my desk to see when I'm free.'

The relief surged through her like a tidal wave, leaving her speechless for several seconds.

'Fine,' she croaked weakly. 'Just give me a ring when you know your timetable.'

'It's going to be a bit hectic for a few days while I catch up on the backlog. I'm hardly going to have time to breathe.' He shook his head.

'Well, you be careful. Your back won't stand much punishment for a while. Make sure you don't sit still for too long. Stop at intervals to move about a bit.' A thought struck her. 'Do you know when the next meeting is going to be at the hospital—or is that one of the things still waiting to be sorted?'

'I've no idea, yet. I'll let you know as soon as I can. Have you heard anything from your Association?'

'Nothing further. Not since we started gathering the figures to sort out the comparative costings.' She shrugged her shoulders, releasing a deep breath. 'It seems all wrong somehow that something as important as providing health-care should all come down to the availability of money.'

'In what way?'

'Almost every way, it seems. The patients I treat have to pay to see me privately, because my treatment is not available on the NHS. Then, when we start investigating how it *can* be provided, it all comes down to expense again. It feels like putting a price-tag on health.'

'It's getting more and more like that from our end, too,' he agreed. 'Every penny has to be accounted for. Don't get me wrong, I'd be horrified if money was being wasted. But sometimes it makes you wonder which the bean-counters would prefer—the ideal solution for the patient, or the cheapest one.'

'But for all that, I bet you wouldn't change your job!' she challenged. 'It's obviously something you find very satisfying.'

'Oh, yes. I wouldn't change jobs, in spite of the frustrations.' He paused. 'Speaking of which. . .' He raised one eyebrow.

'Pardon?' Rebecca had a feeling she had just lost the thread of the conversation.

'I was just talking about frustration.' His voice had grown decidedly husky in the last few moments as he reached out to stroke across the back of her hand with the tip of one lean finger. 'When are you going to let me take you out again?' His eyes lifted from their preoccupation with the movement of his finger over the fine bones of her wrist and fixed on the soft confusion of her dark brown gaze.

'I'm not. . . I mean. . .we can't. Not while you're my patient. It wouldn't be right.' Rebecca felt a sick disappointment settle deep inside. He wasn't going to start the argument again, was he?

'All right,' he capitulated. 'But I hope you realise that I'm only giving up so easily because of my weakened state. I'm just not fit to fight you yet—or is it fight for you?' He paused in mock puzzlement. 'I'll have to try to work it all out when my strength returns.'

His eyes met hers and she was bathed in the heat of the fire she saw burning in their depths. He lifted one hand to trail his knuckles over her cheek before murmuring. 'I think you'd better get ready, because I don't think it's going to take very long.'

He leant forward slowly, his eyes asking a question as they held hers, drawing closer and closer.

Rebecca's silent answer was the involuntary flick of her tongue over her bottom lip.

Alex swooped, his mouth opening over hers to trap a groan between them so that neither knew who had made the sound and neither cared.

In a timeless silence their lips met in a kiss of breathtaking delicacy, that one point their only contact. For Rebecca, all sensation was focused on the warmth of his breath on her cheek, the soft friction of his teeth against the moisture of her tongue, the silky cling of the movement of his lips against hers.

An eternity later he straightened to his full height, breaking the contact between them before stealing a final taste, a final tease of his tongue along the moist pout of her bottom lip.

He stepped back then raised one hand in a brief salute.

'I'll give you a ring. Soon.' His words were a husky promise, his eyes never leaving their contemplation of her mouth.

'He only meant that he was going to phone for his next appointment,' Rebecca lectured herself crossly as she climbed into bed that night.

Her heart had been working overtime all day, every time she thought of that kiss. That wonderful, sensuous, forbidden kiss. And why should she think that his words had been a promise?

She thumped her pillow into shape with a vicious fist and curled up disconsolately under the soft weight of her duvet. She was stupidly reading all sorts of things into a simple. . .

'Hello.' She snatched the phone from its rest and answered breathlessly. 'Alex,' she whispered as the dark magic of his voice spilled over her.

'Who were you expecting?' he growled.

'No one,' she denied shakily.

'No one? When I told you I'd phone?'

'Yes, but that was just to make your next appointment, wasn't it? If you'd like to hang on a minute, I'll just go and get the appointment book. . .'

'Where are you?'

'I'm in bed. . .' She stopped, suddenly realising what she had said.

Alex made a deep groaning sound as if he was in pain.

'What's the matter? Is your back worse?'

'Never mind my back, it's the rest of me I'm more worried about at the moment! Did you have to tell me you were in bed?'

'Well, you asked. . .' Rebecca was amazed to hear the flirtatious note in her voice. She hadn't realised that she knew how. Perhaps it was just a matter of meeting the right person. . .?

'So if I was to ask you what you wear in bed. . .?' He let the sentence trail off suggestively.

'*If* you did, this would probably degenerate into an obscene phone call. In your fragile state of health I hardly think that's wise.' She was having a hard time holding back her laughter. This was the first time she had realised that she could conduct this kind of banter, or what fun it could be.

'Fragile?' he spluttered. 'If I were there I'd show you who's fragile!'

'As your chiropractor, I would be forced to recommend that you wait until you have properly recovered before you think about showing me anything at all!' And the whole ludicrous conversation collapsed in laughter.

'So,' Rebecca murmured into the eventual silence, 'seriously, how are you feeling this evening? Are you still feeling easier?'

'So far, so good,' he confirmed cautiously. 'In fact I have to say I'm amazed by how much of the pain has gone already.'

'You shouldn't be, after sitting-in on all those other patients.'

'That's different. I was only watching them. This time I'm experiencing it for myself.'

Rebecca heard the calm acceptance in his voice and a cautious brightness grew inside her. Perhaps Alex was learning through his own unfortunate experience. Perhaps this was the way he would learn to trust her and the value of her profession.

Their conversation drifted from topic to topic for nearly half an hour, much the same as it had the first time Alex had invited her out for a meal. Rebecca found herself looking forward to the prospect of his speedy recovery. Once he was no longer her patient, she would feel free to accept his first invitation.

She yawned deeply then apologised profusely.

'I didn't realise my conversation was so soporific,' Alex complained.

'It's not!' Rebecca protested, and yawned again. 'I think it's relief of tension.'

'Why?'

'I think, because you sound so much happier, it makes me more relaxed. In fact it's a good job I'm all ready in bed.'

'That's not fair.' It was his turn to protest. 'You're talking about being all ready in bed, and the last thing I'll be is relaxed!'

'I'm sorry,' she murmured softly, her mind buzzing with forbidden images.

'And so you should be, brazen hussy.' He made the words sound like a caress. 'I'm saying goodnight before I disgrace myself. I'll phone again when I know any dates.'

'Night,' she whispered, and went to sleep smiling.

CHAPTER EIGHT

THE world was definitely a wonderful place, Rebecca mused as she floated through her early morning chores.

The sky was brighter, the air was fresher. . .'And I'm going soft in the head!' she muttered in disgust. 'For heaven's sake, it was only one phone call. Don't make such a song and dance about it!' Oh, but it had left her with such hope.

The only problem now was to find enough patience to go about her work in a properly professional manner. It would not do for her to spend her time mooning about waiting for him to call.

As usual, the phone was busy all day with messages from new patients and current ones, but not the one she wanted to hear.

Until late afternoon when there was a familiar knock on the treatment-room door.

Her feet hardly seemed to touch the carpet as she sped to the door.

'Come in, Mr Marshall. You've met Mr Chapman before, haven't you?'

'Thank you, Dr James. Yes. We met about two weeks ago, I think. How have you been?'

'I was doing all right, marvellous, in fact, until my neighbour had a delivery of quick-drying cement just as storm clouds started piling up. Like an idiot, I pitched in to help and nearly put myself back to square one. I've decided to change that old saying to "A friend in need is a flaming nuisance".' He pulled a face as Rebecca settled him in position for treatment.

'I know what you mean,' Alex agreed. 'It always seems a rotten way of being repaid for a good deed—to end up in pain.'

'Just think yourself lucky you haven't finished up like me, needing treatment from Dr James to sort you out,' was his parting shot as he left the room.

'Speaking of treatment,' Alex said in a low voice, 'I took a quick look in the book on my way through and he's the last one this afternoon. Does that mean you'll have time to see me now? I didn't phone because I didn't know what time I could get away.'

'If you don't mind waiting a minute while I complete Mr Chapman's file and make his appointment? Or are you due somewhere else in a hurry?'

'No, I've actually got some time to call my own. Just don't tell anyone or they'll phone me up with another emergency, or some hitch in the paperwork mountain!'

Rebecca escorted Mr Chapman to the reception area and slipped the catch on the front door after he left.

'Oh, Alex, I'm sorry, I should have given you a gown, then you could have been undressing while you waited.'

'That's no problem,' he soothed as he crossed the room towards her. 'It was good just to stand still for a few minutes knowing I didn't have to dash off somewhere.'

He took hold of her elbow and moved her aside so that he could close the door, then led her over to her chair.

'That's better,' he murmured as she sat down rather uncertainly, her pulse-rate suddenly erratic as she caught sight of the strange expression on his face.

'Alex, don't you want to get changed. . .' Her voice faded as he shook his head, his shoulders shrugging to send his charcoal-grey jacket sliding down his arms.

'Alex? What. . .?' He leant forward to place the tip of one finger on her lips.

'Shh. I don't really need a gown, do I?' The expression on his face was wicked and his eyes were molten steel.

He raised both hands to loosen the knot of his striped silk tie, and continued by unbuttoning his pristine white shirt, pausing briefly to pull the tails out of the waistband of his suit trousers.

'Alex! What are you. . .? Why. . .?' The words wouldn't come, her brain was so overloaded with visual stimuli.

Her eyes were everywhere, from the dark whorls of silky hair he had revealed on his broad chest as he stripped away his shirt, to the lean elegance of his feet as he removed his dark socks.

Rebecca couldn't believe what she was seeing, couldn't believe what he was doing.

Was this really Alexander Marshall the forbidding, humourless monolith who had watched her every move to catch her out in some heinous misdeed?

Impossible.

This man watched her, it was true, but he was charting the flush of arousal she could feel rising up her throat and spreading across her face. This man was as aware as she was that she had just folded her arms because it was the only acceptable way of supporting the swelling weight of her tingling breasts.

The sharp rasp of his zipper drew her eyes, first to the front of his trousers where the dark hair proliferated over the top of the white pants visible as the opening gaped. Then, as he paused, her eyes were drawn upwards to witness the flush which appeared along his cheekbones.

Abruptly he turned, and in one swift series of moves

had discarded his trousers on top of the pile of clothes on the chair beside him and was lying face down on the couch.

Rebecca remained in her seat, convinced that her shaking legs would never support her. Her hands, too, were trembling, as she noticed when she put one out to pick up her pen.

Her fine analytical brain suddenly switched on.

He had been enjoying himself taunting her, until. . . until it had come to the point where he had to remove his trousers. Then he'd apparently lost his nerve—or had he?

What if. . .? What if he had been equally as aroused as she had? That would explain why he had turned away so sharply. And if that was the case, it was only fair that he should be dealt some of his own medicine.

Rebecca found that her deliberations had steadied her hands. Her legs, too, had recovered enough to carry her over to the couch where Alex now lay still and quiet. Only the residual flush on the back of his neck remained as evidence of his discomposure.

'How has your back been since I treated you?' she was proud of the steadiness of her voice.

'Better.' His voice was muffled by his position—at least, she gave him the benefit of the doubt that that was the reason.

'How about your degree of mobility?'

'That's better, too.' This time he had lifted his head slightly to speak.

What she could see of his face wore a rather puzzled expression, and Rebecca could have chortled with glee.

He had obviously been expecting her to make some comment about his teasing; was waiting for her to say something—anything. That realisation made her more determined than ever to pay him back in his own coin.

For the rest of his appointment time Rebecca behaved with impeccable professionalism towards him. Not by a single word did she refer to his earlier performance. Her voice and manner were as calm and soothing as they always were when dealing with patients.

'The spasm over your right sacroiliac area is much less, isn't it?' she kept up her usual flow of informative conversation as she progressed. 'And the secondary problem in your thoracic region has virtually disappeared.' She had him take a deep breath and release it as she adjusted his back.

'Did you use the ice?'

'Mm-hmm,' he mumbled his agreement into the headpiece. 'I wasn't looking forward to putting something so cold on my back, but the relief was wonderful.'

Gradually, she felt the tension leave his body until, by the end of the treatment, he was totally relaxed.

Now, she thought to herself, we'll just see how you like this.

When she had been training, one of her fellow students had been a qualified masseuse. Rebecca had attended her abbreviated tutorials on massage technique purely out of interest, as it did not form part of her chiropractic course.

This would be the first time she had used her skill since she had learned it.

She warmed some baby oil between the palms of her hands and then ran them over his back to spread it in an even layer over his muscles. Then she started to work her way through the muscle groups, concentrating on visualising the relevant pages in her anatomy books to avoid the pitfall Alex had discovered—that of arousing herself at the same time!

It was nearly five minutes before he finally reached the stage where he couldn't stand any more.

'You witch!' he growled, his muffled voice hardly recognisable in the husky roar. 'You're doing it on purpose, aren't you?'

'Doing what?' she asked innocently, moving quickly aside so that his grasping hand couldn't trap her.

'Is this treatment part of your normal repertoire?' He turned his head to glare at her as she continued to work the long muscles on the backs of his powerful thighs.

Daringly, she allowed her fingers to trail up the insides of his legs, travelling just a little higher with each sweep.

'Enough!' he bellowed hoarsely. 'I can't turn over because of my back injury.'

Instantly penitent, Rebecca moved forward to help him move—and discovered just too late that it was merely a cunning ploy.

'Gotcha!' he gloated as his hands trapped both of her wrists like manacles.

Using the contact as leverage, Alex rolled on to his side and swung his legs around to sit himself up.

'I think,' he started speaking slowly and deliberately, 'that anyone who would taunt a weak, defenceless patient in such an underhand way deserves everything they get!' His final words were hardly more than a whisper. The puffs of breath were warm and moist against her mouth as he pulled inexorably on her hands to bring her lips down to his.

'Alex.' Their lips touched fleetingly as she pleaded with him. 'Alex, no. We mustn't.'

'You should have thought of the consequences before you started your little game.'

'But you started it!' she wailed, and he took advantage of her open mouth to stroke the top of his tongue across her bottom lip.

He drew his head back, his eyes focused on her mouth. Unconsciously, her own tongue emerged to taste the trace of himself he had left there.

With a groan he leant forward again to take possession of her lips, his hands releasing her wrists to encircle her body and draw her between the spread of his thighs.

For long murmurous moments that contact was enough. Her newly liberated hands had found a more comfortable position clasped among the silky darkness of the hair on the back of his head, while his were fully occupied stroking the length of her back.

'Becca,' he whispered against her mouth, making the single word sound like a prayer.

Convulsively, he tightened his arms about her until their bodies made full contact.

For the first time Rebecca was made graphically aware of his arousal, and the realisation caused her to tense warily in his arms.

'Alex?' she breathed uncertainly.

'Mmm?' He angled his head to take her lips in a kiss that seemed fathoms deep. It was almost enough to overrule her doubts until his hand swept down to her hips to pull their bodies into intimate alignment.

'Alex, no. We can't. You're still my patient.' She put one hand up to his mouth to prevent him kissing her again, but he simply transferred his attention to the sensitive skin of her palm.

'Alex!' She still had one hand buried in his hair and she tightened in into a fist.

'Ow!' His eyes flew open in pained shock. 'What was that for?'

'To make you stop,' Rebecca said in a small voice.

'There are other ways of getting my attention.'

'I know. I tried, but. . .' Stupidly, she felt herself blushing and she tilted her head forward.

'You can't have tried very hard. Perhaps it's because you don't really mean it.'

'Yes. . . No. . . I mean. . . Oh!' she took a deep breath to clear her muddled thoughts and began again, all too conscious of his sardonic expression.

'Yes, I do mean it. We must stop, you know we must,' she appealed. 'It isn't ethical for us to. . .' She felt her cheeks flame again.

'And what do you suggest I do about this?' He pulled her against himself again. 'It's your fault I'm in this state.'

'It's your fault, too. You started it with that striptease.'

'I only did that out of devilment after that phone call last night.' He shifted his position against the couch slightly and Rebecca realised how highly aroused he still was. 'Becca,' he groaned, 'this will have to be one of the fastest recovery times in chiropractic history or I don't know how I'm going to survive! Now, stand still for goodness' sake.'

'I'm sorry,' she murmured penitently in a small voice.

'So you ought to be.' There was a slightly sharp tone to his voice. 'Didn't your mother ever warn you it could be dangerous to play games like that?'

'Actually, no, she didn't.' Rebecca's tone had cooled too. 'She was rather busy when I reached that stage, so she handed me a selection of anatomy and physiology books. Needless to say, they were rather short on details like the emotional aspects of arousal.'

'But you're twenty-four now. Are you trying to tell

me that you haven't had any experience since puberty?'
his voice was scornful.

'Not a lot,' Rebecca answered baldly, her chin
coming up in defiance. 'I had my nose kept pretty close
to the grindstone at school and then, when I went to
AECC, I had too much to prove to waste time on
socialising.'

'I'm sorry.' He was apologetic. 'It's not fair for me
to take my frustration out on you.'

He grasped her shoulders in the palms of his hands
and pushed firmly.

'If you would like to sit yourself down at your desk
and write up the last of your case-notes, I'll get myself
dressed again. This time I'll manage to do it better
without an audience!'

Although Rebecca was grateful for his attempt at
humour, she could tell even without the lightning
glance she had taken at his lower body that he was still
not comfortable.

Nor was he very pleased with her continued refusal
to do anything about deepening their relationship while
he was her patient.

Her guilt at her part in his discomfort made her feel
awkward with him, and she was glad when he made
the excuse of a backlog of work to leave shortly after.

She was curled up in the corner of her couch clutching
a cup of coffee and blaming herself for the strained
atmosphere between Alex and herself when the doorbell rang.

'Alex!' she whispered and, depositing her coffee-cup
on the nearest flat surface, she flew to the door on
winged feet.

'Mother! Father! What's the matter? What are you

doing here?' She couldn't have been more surprised if she had seen aliens from Mars on her doorstep.

'Ahem.' Her father cleared his throat. 'Is it a good time for a visit, or would you rather we phoned another time?'

Her father? Asking politely?

'No. I mean, yes, come in. . .' She stepped back and held the door wider. 'Walk straight through into the sitting-room. Have you got time for a cup of coffee?'

One small corner of her brain was conscious that she was behaving just like a flustered hostess with unexpected guests.

'Is there something wrong?' she repeated anxiously.

Her mother was seated at one end of the settee but her father remained standing until she remembered his old-fashioned manners and sat herself in the armchair.

'No. Nothing wrong, exactly.' He glanced across at his wife as he sat down.

'Your father and I were talking, and we realised that we'd never seen the inside of your house. . .or the practice. So, as we were coming this way, we thought we'd see if it was convenient. . .?'

Rebecca was stunned into silence. This was the first interest they had shown in where she was living, let alone where she was working.

'Did you want some coffee?' She felt the need to get up and move. 'It won't take a moment, and then I could show you round.'

'That would be lovely, dear. Do you need any help?'

'No,' she confirmed hastily. 'If you wait here, it won't take long,' and she escaped into the kitchen.

As she took out her favourite Portmeirion cups and saucers and put them on the matching tray she realised that her hands were shaking. What did this visit mean?

Was it a new phase in the campaign to bring her

back into the fold of "real" medicine? Or was it the start of a whole new chapter in their relationship?

She carried the tray through, conscious that the rattle of cups against saucers betrayed her trembling.

'Mother. Do you still take sugar in coffee?'

'No, dear. We both decided to give it up when weight started to creep on. It doesn't do for doctors to tell their patients what to do if they aren't obeying the rules themselves!'

'Not that self-righteousness makes the coffee taste any better without sugar!' her father grumbled. 'I don't miss potatoes in my diet, but I do miss the sugar in my coffee, especially at the end of a meal.'

They sat silently sipping for a few moments while they avoided each other's eyes by looking around the room.

'You've made this room very comfortable, Rebecca. Are you sure you don't need any of your furniture from home? It's such a price to buy new these days.'

'No, Mother, this is fine for me. I managed to find most of what I wanted quite cheaply second-hand and did the refinishing myself in the evenings while I was doing my graduate year. Then, when I found this place, there wasn't much left to get.'

'How did you manage the financing?' Her father had the grace to look a little uncomfortable when he asked.

'The BCA, my professional association, were able to put me in touch with someone. Apparently there are various schemes now to help newly qualified chiropractors set up in practice. The biggest problem is the Catch-22 situation. You can't get a mortgage without proof of income, and you can't start earning to provide the proof without the property to start earning in!'

'But you managed to get it all sorted out?'

'Yes, with a lot of luck and an understanding bank manager!'

'Do they still exist? I thought they were extinct!' His humour was a little heavy-handed, but it was a start.

Rebecca finished her coffee and put her cup back on the tray.

'Did you want to see the rest of it? I haven't quite finished in the bathroom and the little boxroom. . .'

'We'd love to,' her mother declared, and they followed her out into the hallway.

'It's surprisingly spacious, isn't it,' was her father's comment when they had finished the tour of her own accommodation.

'I suppose that's one of the benefits of having home and practice in the same building. I wanted to get something big enough for the practice to be all on the ground floor—for the sake of the patients who have difficulty with stairs—and that meant that I ended up with extra space for myself.'

'Have you decided what you'll do with the room?'

'I'll probably lose it when the practice expands enough to take in an associate. Then I'll move myself completely upstairs.'

'But what will happen if you decide to get married?' her mother's voice broke in. 'You won't have any room for a family.'

'I'll worry about that when the time comes.' Rebecca was grimly aware of the heavy lump which had appeared in her chest as she was reminded of Alex and her fleeting hopes. 'There's no prospect for a long time yet.'

She saw the look which passed between her parents and wondered briefly if they had started thinking about the prospect of grandparenthood.

They're in for a long wait, she thought sadly. The

only man she wanted to be the father of her children; the only one she had even found who could set her blood on fire, found it impossible to trust her.

She knew there was a reason; something which had happened in the past which was like an unscaleable wall inside him. Until he realised that the wall had to come down before their relationship could flourish, she was wasting her time. She shook her head at her conclusions.

'Rebecca?' She had the feeling that it wasn't the first time her mother had spoken.

'I'm sorry, Mother. I was just woolgathering.' She squared her shoulders. 'Do you have time to have a look around the practice too?'

Expecting a polite refusal with the excuse of pressure of work, she was amazed when they both seemed so eager.

This was strange. It was the longest she had spent in her parents' company without the outbreak of a full-scale war in more than six years. What did it mean? What was going on? It wasn't many weeks since her father had publicly denigrated her choice of profession—in front of Alex.

Uneasily, she took them through into the X-ray room and then showed them the automatic developer she had installed behind a light-proof enclosure.

'This is all new equipment.' Her father was amazed. 'It's probably every bit as good as the ones we've got at St Augustine's.'

'Actually, it's the same make,' Rebecca confirmed quietly.

'Surely you could have got something second-hand instead of going to all this expense?'

'I decided to start as I mean to go on. I provide a

first-rate service, and for that I need first-rate equipment,' she stated with quiet pride.

'But how have you financed it all? Don't tell me,' he added when he caught the edge of her smile and they finished in unison 'an understanding bank manager!'

Later, his smile died and he asked seriously, 'Are you managing all right? Do you need any help?'

This was another first, Rebecca thought. When she had turned down the place at medical school, he had told her in no uncertain terms that she was on her own.

It had been hard, but her determination had seen her through.

'No, Father. I'm all right.'

'Are you sure? It could be a loan, if you wanted to keep your independence. Just to tide you over?'

'Thanks for the offer.' Rebecca could hear the tightness in her throat as she forced the words out. 'But I'm over the worst of it now. The practice is building up well, and the bank manager has stopped mopping his brow!'

She had made a joke of it, but how much better it would have been if the offer had been made when she had really been desperate for help.

Now, she had the satisfaction of knowing that she had succeeded on her own terms, but that had done nothing to cement the adult relationship between herself and her parents.

Perhaps they had come to the same realisation. Perhaps that was why they had decided to visit?

The only way she could find out was to ask, even if it meant ruffling the surprisingly calm waters of this unexpected call.

'Was there any special reason for coming today?' She had always believed in taking the bull by the horns.

'Not really. . .' her father broke the sudden silence then paused as her mother fixed him with a fierce gaze.

'Actually, dear, it was a combination of things,' she explained. 'When we picked you up to go to the dinner, there wasn't time to come in. We both said afterwards that we would like to see what you had done inside but, well, we weren't sure whether we would be welcome. . .' The unfinished sentence sounded hesitant—a most unusual thing for her perennially positive-sounding parents.

'Of course you would have been welcome. I've enjoyed showing you round. It's like showing off— look what I've done—isn't it?'

'Well,' her father explained, 'it wasn't until one of the other consultants in Orthopaedics was telling me about your input on one of his patients, and then a couple of the others put their oars in about other cases referred to them through some of your collegues, that it got me thinking.

'They all stressed how helpful your profession had been, especially in helping the patients to cut through some of the red tape.'

'I'm even coming across it in my department,' her mother broke in. 'I wouldn't have thought your profession would have any contact with ENT, but I've had a couple of referrals for screening in connection with Costen's.'

'We were talking about it this lunchtime,' her father took up the reins again, 'and we were all saying how professional their approach had been. None of the ranting and outlandish claims of some of the "fringe" people.' He had the grace to look a little abashed at his use of the same words he had used to describe her choice of profession. This change of heart was going to take a little time to get used to.

'I know it's always going to be a case of "too little, too late", dear, but do you think it will be possible for us to learn to tolerate each other, if nothing else?'

'Oh, Dad!' she reverted to his childhood name as she threw her arms around his shoulders. 'We'll work it out, between us.'

At the hesitant touch on her arm she turned slightly to include her mother in the embrace.

It was nearly an hour and another cup of coffee later that they stood by the front door saying their farewells.

'I still maintain you would have made a first-class doctor, you know,' her father rumbled, 'but if you're happy with what you've chosen, at least you're making a first-class job of it.'

'Thomas,' his wife admonished. 'Trust you to put a damper on things.'

'Rebecca knows I've always spoken my own mind. She's too much a chip off the old block to believe that I've changed my point of view completely, so what difference does it make?'

'None,' Rebecca agreed. 'Provided you understand that being a chip off the old block means that I'm just as likely to stick to my guns.' They all groaned at the old habit she had of mixing her metaphors.

Not wanting to lose the opportunity to build on the unexpected empathy, Rebecca made a rapid invitation.

'As soon as I've finished the bathroom, I'd thought of having a house-warming party. Just a few people for a drink and a buffet meal. Would you like invitations when I know the date?'

'It depends how busy we'll. . .' Rebecca saw her father receive a swift jab from her mother's elbow.

'We'd love to receive an invitation,' she confirmed warmly. 'We'll do our best to make sure we're free that

evening. After all, there must be some perks to senior-
ity even if it's only getting to rearrange evenings off!'

As she watched their car leave, Rebecca couldn't
stop herself wrapping her arms around her ribs and
squeezing. She could feel the huge grin on her face,
and suddenly couldn't wait to tell someone what had
happened.

Alex!

The first name to come to mind, and the only one
who she really wanted to tell.

It wasn't that she had full acceptance from her
parents of her choice of career; her father's comment
had shown her that. At least, now, there was a chance
for them to build a satisfactory relationship based on a
degree of mutual respect.

If only she could achieve the same with Alex.

The phone rang three times before it was answered.
Then, although it was Alex's voice, it was a recording
on his answering machine, asking her to leave her
name and number.

She paused in thought while she waited for the
inevitable bleep and then put the handset down without
leaving a message.

It was Alex she wanted to speak to, his voice she
wanted to hear while she told him about the momen-
tous changes which had happened out of the blue.

Where was Alex?

Surely at this time of night he would have been at
home—unless he was out with someone. . . Sophie?

No. He had sounded so scathing about their former
relationship that she knew there was no chance of the
other woman getting her hooks into Alex twice.

'Alex,' she murmured softly into the quiet dark of
her bedroom. 'Where are you when I need to talk
to you?'

The little voice inside her head continued her thoughts.

What difference would it make to his attitudes when he heard about her parents' change of heart? Would he, too, become more accepting, or would the secret he kept locked away inside him still keep them apart?

As she curled up around her pillow, she found herself replaying in her mind the events in her treatment-room the last time he had come for treatment.

'Hurry up and get better,' she muttered, as she felt the early stages of arousal creeping inexorably through her. 'I don't know how long I can hold myself back!' She heard the soft echo of her drowsy chuckle, and shifted to a more comfortable position and yawned.

I just wish he would talk to me about—whatever it is, her thoughts continued silently. Then I'll know what it is keeping us apart. . . She shifted position again, conscious of the silky brush of her skin against her skimpy ivory teddy.

If we don't manage to get ourselves sorted out soon. . . I'm probably going to become a victim of spontaneous combustion, the thought drifted on one stage further, but if we do sort things out. . .if Alex finds that he loves me even half as much as I love him. . .I think we'll both go up in flames. . .

CHAPTER NINE

'DR JAMES?' It was an efficient-sounding female voice on the other end of the phone. 'This is Mr Marshall's secretary.'

Rebecca's heart gave an extra thump before it settled into rhythm.

'He asked me to tell you that it's important he sees you as soon as possible.'

'Pardon?' Would he have entrusted such a personal message to his secretary?

'It's something about these trials.' Rebecca's heart sank back down into her boots. 'I need to know when you're free so that I can book a time for you all to get together at the hospital.'

'Let me get my appointment book open,' Rebecca muttered, fighting the urge to kick something. 'Let me see. . . I can be free to come over by about half-past four today, if it's really urgent, or will tomorrow morning be soon enough?'

'I think this afternoon will probably be best, but I'll get back to you if it's any different.'

'Will we be in the same conference-room?'

'I won't know that until later. Shall I leave a message for you at Reception if I don't speak to you in the meantime?'

The rest of the morning Rebecca was conscious of a gradual build-up of tension—not that she allowed it to affect her treatment of her patients.

What was the urgent meeting about, and why had Alex not been in contact with her himself?

During the weeks since they had met they had been drawn closer and closer to each other in spite of the constraints of their doctor-patient relationship, until their last encounter had almost reached explosion point.

Surely Alex was missing her company as much as she was missing his; he must be wanting to speak to her, hear her voice. The compulsion she felt was too strong to be one-sided.

The only problem was the fact that he still didn't trust her, and she knew that this distrust was deeply rooted.

What would she do if the roots went too deep for him to remove?

There was a message waiting for her at Reception with directions to Alex's consulting-room. They were very straightforward, but Rebecca found her feet dragging unaccountably the closer she got.

She was longing to see Alex again, but something was telling her that this was not going to be an enjoyable meeting, and she was loath to do anything to spoil the small measure of happiness she was hanging on to.

'Come in.' His deep voice beckoned, and she took a deep breath before pushing the door open.

He looked up briefly, his polished steel gaze transfixing her before he returned his attention to the spread of papers on the desk.

'Can you find youself a seat?' he asked distractedly. 'I'm sorry about this——' he gestured at the mess with his free hand as he scrawled a notation on one of the sheets '—but life has been a little more hectic than usual the last couple of days.'

He drew one hand down his face wearily and slid it round to massage the back of his neck.

'My secretary tried to catch you to warn you that the meeting would be better tomorrow, but you'd already left to come here.' As he closed one file and opened another he darted a glance at her. 'Have you got time to wait while I plough my way through the last of these?'

He had looked bad enough when his back had been at its worst, but now he looked worn out. What had he been doing to himself since she had last seen him?

She sat herself quietly in one of the chairs beside his desk and prepared to wait. There was no way she was going to leave without finding out what had been happening—both to the trials and to Alex himself.

At the next shuffle of papers she asked, 'Is Ellen going to join us later?'

'No.' He looked up, the expression in his eyes shuttered as they met hers. 'She knows what it's all about, so there's no point in her being here.' He paused as if deciding whether to continue then shook his head and looked down again. 'I should be finished with this in about five minutes, then I can concentrate. . .' His words trailed into silence as his pen started moving again.

She watched idly as the broad nib made slashing black marks on the paper, trying to isolate the strange feelings building up inside her.

Finally, he screwed the top on the pen and threw it on the top of the pile.

'Done, at last.' He grimaced as he stretched his arms above his head. 'It's a good job my chiropractor hasn't seen what I've been up to since she treated me last. She'd be surprised how well my back has stood up to it.'

'Why?' She raised one eyebrow. 'What *have* you been up to?'

The teasing smile on his face died suddenly. 'Too much standing around,' he said cryptically.

He swung his chair round and walked over to the window where he turned to lean his hips against the edge of the windowsill. He was silhouetted against the sky, his shoulders impossibly broad and powerful, but the light behind his head meant that the expressions on his face were indistinct.

'Alex, what is this all about? Your receptionist seemed to think it was urgent that a meeting was arranged, but when I get here you're up to your eyes in paperwork and Ellen isn't coming.' She turned slightly in her chair so that she was facing him squarely. 'So, what's going on?'

There was a pause and she saw his shoulders rise as he breathed in deeply and then released the air in a sigh.

'The trials been put on hold,' he said quietly.

There was a long silence while Rebecca tried to absorb the import of the bald statement.

'Why?' she finally managed. 'What have you done?' Her mind suddenly filled with rage, she sprang out of her seat and flew around his desk to confront him.

'I don't know how you've managed it, but I think it's despicable.' She planted one fist on each hip and glared up at him. This close, she could see his face and the arrested expression on it. 'Tell me,' she challenged. 'Tell me what you've done to have the trials halted. Ohhh! I knew you didn't trust complementary therapies right from the start, but you know how important the trials are, not just to me personally, but to the profession and the patients. I thought at least you would have the honesty to admit the benefit you've received from it and be willing to let others share in that help.'

She wrapped her arms tightly around herself to disguise the violent shaking which had started inside her, battling with the deep well of hurt that he could have treated her this way.

'I thought my father was bad, with his blinkered views, but he's from an older, less tolerant generation. Even he had to admit he was wrong when the evidence was presented to him.

'They came over last night to talk to me.' It was heartbreaking to be telling him like this. 'It was the first time we've talked since I turned down the place at medical school, but at least he was always open with his disapproval.

'But you?' she drew in a gasping breath. 'You sneaked around behind my back. . .'

'You didn't listen.' He interrupted harshly. Each word was like an icicle. 'I said, the trials have been put. . .on. . .hold.'

Doubt swirled around her head like an ominous cloud.

'And. . .?' she prompted. 'What does that mean?'

'The normal reaction would have been to ask why, or until when, don't you think? So many different ways to react.' He shook his head and walked over to his desk where he sank slowly into his chair.

'Not you, though,' he skewered her with his eyes. 'You immediately decide that it's all a plot against you. What an ego!' His scorn withered her, and her throat was too dry to allow her to speak.

'For your information, I asked my secretary to call you in so that I could tell you what was happening myself. I thought you might be upset to learn about it in an impersonal way such as a phone call from a stranger.

'For my pains I have been subjected to a completely unwarranted attack on my ethics and personal moral conduct.' She had never seen him as icily angry as this.

Rebecca felt the burning sensation start at the back of her eyes as she realised that this time her habit of fighting her corner had gone too far. This time her salvo had been wide of the mark and had done serious damage.

She blinked hard, determined not to let a single tear fall although her eyes were brimming.

He continued in a coldly dispassionate voice. 'The trials have been put on hold because there was insufficient information about the costings in the physiotherapy department.'

'And that's it?' her incredulous voice sounded scratchy.

'That's it,' he confirmed. 'Without those figures we can't make any projections about comparative cost-effectiveness. Once they've been collated, the trials can continue.'

'H—how long will that take?'

'How long is a piece of string?' he rubbed his eyes wearily. 'I'm sorry. I'm not at my best this afternoon.' He dropped his hand to focus slightly bloodshot eyes on her.

'I was called in to consult about a crash victim late last night. Skull fracture.' He shook his head. 'She died at four this morning.' His expression was utterly bleak. 'She was only twenty. . .'

Rebecca waited, knowing from the tension surrounding him that there was more.

'She looked just like my sister.' His voice had a strange hollow sound.

His sister? What sister?

Rebecca's sharp intake of breath seemed to snap him out of his strange mood. Before she could frame her question, he started to speak briskly, reverting to the original topic of conversation as though regretting the lapse into a personal topic.

'The delay on these trials is a bit of a godsend for me. I've got a series of lectures coming up and some research of my own to complete. I'm desperately short of time at the moment, especially having to take a week off for ill-health.' He drew the corners of his mouth down in a grimace.

'Touch wood, that seems much better now, particularly since I put that heel-lift in my shoe.' He flicked her a half smile but she noticed that it didn't reach his eyes. 'I must admit that I didn't believe it would do any good, but in the interests of scientific investigation I gave it a go.

'I would never have lasted out the night if you hadn't suggested it. Thank you.' There could be no doubt of his sincerity but there was no warmth in his voice, and Rebecca felt her throat closing up again.

Putting out one shaky hand she found the back of a chair and moved unobtrusively across to lean against it, hiding the fact behind the folds of her silky skirt.

'That's the other thing I had to remember to tell you. I won't be able to book any further treatment sessions, at least not until I've cleared the decks a bit.' He avoided meeting her eyes by fixing his gaze on his hands.

'But. . .' Rebecca felt as if she'd been dealt a death blow.

'That's no reflection on your treatment.' He added quickly. 'I realise that there is no way I could be up on my feet if you hadn't treated me, and I know that I should complete the treatment, but, dammit, there just aren't enough hours in the day!' His frustration was evident in his clenched fist and the tension in his jaw.

'I'll ring for an appointment as soon as I can see daylight beyond the mountain of research notes I've got to organise.'

'Don't forget to set an egg-timer,' she whispered huskily.

'An egg-timer?' The outlandish suggestion finally brought his questioning gaze to hers. 'What on earth for?'

'An alarm clock would do. Just to make sure you get up and walk around at intervals, or you'll seize up again.'

'Thanks for the tip.' He smiled bleakly. 'I was dreading the possibility of going through all that misery again.'

'Well——' Rebecca took the first step towards the door, her eyes fixed longingly on the rumpled darkness of his hair. She clenched her fingers to conquer the yearning to run them through the silky strands just once more.

'I'd better let you get on with all that work, then.' Her tear-roughened voice was subdued, the ache inside her robbing her off all animation.

'I'm glad your parents have come round at last,' he offered.

'Oh, it's not an unconditional acceptance, but it's a start. At least we're talking now, which is much better than the open warfare existing between us before.' She turned back at the door to face him. 'They said it was other consultants at St Augustine's who persuaded them they were wrong. I wish I knew which ones.'

'Why? What does it matter?' His dark lashes dropped to shutter his expression.

'I'd like the chance to thank them for giving me back my family.' She gave a slightly embarrassed shrug. 'That sounds rather over-dramatic, I know, but. . . They were never very demonstrative even when I was small, but I hadn't realised until we were finally speaking how much I'd missed them.' She shook her head as her eyes brimmed with tears. 'Silly, isn't it? And at my age.'

'You're never too old to appreciate having a family, or to miss them when they're not there.' That strange hollow sound was back in his voice again.

He leant forward suddenly to gather up the pile of papers.

'As I said, I'll be in touch about another appointment as soon as I can. In the meantime, I'm going to take it very carefully.'

Rebecca knew when she was being dismissed and with a brief murmur of 'Bye, Alex,' and a last view of his broad shoulders outlined against the back of his chair, his head bent once again to his paperwork, she closed the door behind her.

Afterwards, she was never quite sure how she got home safely. She certainly didn't remember driving herself.

The next thing she did remember clearly was sitting at the little table in the kitchen and staring numbly out of the window at the grey clouds piling up one on top of another.

'At least the weather is going to be as miserable as I am,' she heard herself say out loud, her voice a shaky travesty of its normal self.

With that, a double storm broke, the rain lashing furiously at the window while she buried her face in her arms and sobbed her heart out across the kitchen table. They raged unabated for what seemed like hours, a noisy combination of heartbreak and impotent fury.

Finally, the two storms blew themselves out together, leaving their survivors limp and battered.

Rebecca took herself off to the bathroom to splash her face with handfuls of cold water, grimacing at her reflection in the mirror.

'Rudolf the red-nosed reindeer has arrived a little early this year,' she mumbled, sounding as if she was just going down with a heavy cold. She had known how awful she would look; it was one of the curses of being a pale-skinned redhead.

At least her face would have returned to normal by the time she was next due to see anyone. She couldn't be nearly so confident of the state of her heart.

'I'm a survivor,' she told herself. 'I'm going to keep telling myself until I believe it. I'm a survivor.'

She gave herself a determined nod in the mirror and marched back into the kitchen to make herself a meal she didn't want and forced herself to eat it.

'You've got responsibilities now, my girl. You've got to keep yourself fit and well so that you can treat your patients. You can't afford to go into a Victorian decline over a man, even if he is the one you fell in love with.'

She felt her eyes brim with tears again and sniffed hard.

'Enough of that!' she scolded herself. 'You were only saying yesterday that you're going to have a party as soon as you've finished the bathroom and boxroom. Well, now you're going to have some unexpected free time to get on with it. Make the most of it.'

Her pep-talk must have done the trick, because she woke up the next morning filled with determination. Nothing was going to get her down.

She wrote herself a list of decorating supplies and found that her first efforts at tiling a splashback over the bathroom sink were a good omen.

From then on, she filled every waking hour with work of one kind or another.

During the day she was becoming busier and busier. It seemed that the local GPs weren't waiting for the results of the hospital trials. Increasing numbers were referring patients to her. Some who were fund-holders had actually spoken to her about the possibility of working out some sort of financial scheme to help the less wealthy afford to come to her.

She had also been delighted to receive an enquiry from a local factory asking her to give a talk on prevention of back trouble which had been followed up by an approach to go on retainer for the employees to visit her as part of a health insurance scheme.

The only problem was, every time something like that happened, the first thing that crossed her mind was that she wanted to share the excitement with Alex.

Everywhere she went, everything she did, her thoughts seemed to return inevitably to Alex Marshall. One day she even found herself childishly doodling 'Rebecca Marshall' on the edge of one of her lists of 'Things to do'.

She told herself that keeping busy was the answer, and pushed herself harder and harder until even she could see the dark circles appearing under her eyes.

'Enough!' she shouted at herself when she caught sight of herself in the full-length mirror in the treat-ment-room. 'So, he hasn't called to make an appoint-ment, and his mother isn't coming to see me unless she needs to. That only means that no one will be talking about him, reminding me about him.' As if she could forget.

She looked at herself again.

Since that awful meeting at the hospital she had lost nearly half a stone in weight.

'Whoever said a woman could never be too thin obviously hadn't got me in mind. I look like a scarecrow!' She caught hold of a handful of loose material on a skirt that used to fit beautifully.

She sat down on the side of the treatment couch and finally admitted the truth to herself. She felt empty without Alex.

All the frantic activity, all the new patients, all the new contacts meant nothing. They were just a way of filling the day from when she got up until she went to bed.

It was when she went to bed that her mind really came alive, painting fantasy pictures in her dreams. Pictures in which she and Alex were working together on the decorating of her house, spending time together while they ate and talked and made love.

And they did make love.

Every night, in her dreams, she and Alex made wild, passionate love. So vivid was her imagination that when she woke each morning the first thing she did was reach out to touch him. But he was never there.

Would never be there.

If only she had not laid down her ultimatum. Oh, she knew it was the letter of the law as far as professional ethics was concerned, but she had met Alex as a fellow professional before he had become her patient.

Who would it have hurt if they had allowed themselves to become closer—to follow their mutual desire for a full relationship?

Was it all her own fault that he hadn't contacted her? Did he regret knowing her?

Would she ever get over wondering what it would have been like if they had gone to bed together; if she had experienced the passion of a flesh and blood Alex instead of the shadowy phantom who inhabited her dreams?

The final questions which haunted her thoughts were the ones which robbed her of her appetite. Would she ever find a man to put in his place? Was there another man who could fill the gap left in her life and her heart by the absence of Alex Marshall?

Matthew Pryce was clowning around in his own inimitable fashion at the end of his treatment.

'Fair Doctor, by your leave, I'll hie me hence and darken your door no more!' He sketched an elaborate bow, doffing an imaginary cap in the process.

'Until the next time you have a fight with some scenery or overfill your suitcase,' Rebecca returned drily.

'Yea, verily!' he agreed, hand theatrically over heart. 'For which I beg pardon, many time.' His bright blue eyes were full of laughter.

'Give it a rest, Matthew. It gets a bit wearing at the end of a long day.'

'Sorry, old thing.' He tried his well-practised grin on her. 'You know how hyper I get when I'm winding up for a performance. Speaking of which, I really appreciate your fitting me in at short notice like this, or I'd never have been able to go on tonight.' He grimaced wryly. 'I know our motto is supposed to be "the show must go on", but without you jumping on my back, I wouldn't have been putting one foot in front of the other, never mind romping around on stage for a couple of hours.'

Rebecca gave him a few last-minute suggestions to

tide him over until his next treatment, then escorted him to the door.

She found herself laughing heartily as he went into a perfectly awful parody of Romeo's famous soliloquy. He ended his ham performance with a bear-hug and a resounding kiss that was very much more noise than substance, as befitted any stage kiss.

'Thanks again for the treatment, dear heart. As ever, it'll keep me going until I can't stay away from you any longer!' and he kissed her fervently again, missing her mouth by a good quarter-inch while managing to sound as if he was making a meal of her.

'I'm sorry if I'm intruding.'

The surge of joy which welled upwards inside Rebecca at the sound of that deep voice had to fight with the quiver of apprehension which slid down her spine. There had been no sign of apology in the icy words.

Of all the moments for Alex to turn up, it had to be when Matthew was playing the fool.

CHAPTER TEN

'HELLO,' Matthew was irrepressible. 'Do you need the doc to climb all over you, too?'

Rebecca's heart sank as she saw the frozen disdain on Alex's face.

'She'll soon sort you out, mate. She's a very special lady. I don't know what I'd do without her.' He turned back to Rebecca and gave her a final squeeze.

'Are you coming this evening, or shall we meet up in the pub later?'

'I'm not sure, Matthew.' Rebecca glanced across at Alex, battered by the waves of disapproval flooding over her. 'It depends on——'

'It depends on how long her meeting takes with me.' Alex cut across her words brutally, his animosity towards Matthew almost a living entity.

'Well, then, love, take care of yourself.' He walked jauntily towards his car and climbed in, blowing Rebecca a flamboyant kiss as he departed.

As the sound of his car faded into the distance a deathly silence fell.

Rebecca longed to turn towards Alex, to fill her eyes with his presence, but dreaded facing the reality. Her hands curled tightly into fists so that she could feel her nails cutting into the soft flesh of her palms.

'Would it be possible to go inside?' Alex requested tightly.

The tension in his voice achieved the impossible and Rebecca raised her eyes to meet his. They were as cold and hard as granite and she shivered as she turned and led the way towards the door.

She stumbled over the threshold, her heart filled with sick misery.

The door slammed shut behind her, the sudden sound startling her into turning to face him.

He seemed to fill the room, his height and breadth a menacing indication of his strength and power.

'I hardly think that display could be classed as appropriate behaviour for a professional in your position?' The barb went home with a vengeance and all the colour drained from Rebecca's cheeks.

With the speed of a pouncing leopard Alex had her by the shoulders and forced her back against the wall.

'So much for your principles and ethics,' he snarled.

'I *beg* your pardon,' she managed to wheeze, stunned almost breathless by his actions.

'All *I* was trying to do was ask you out for a meal and you turned me down flat. Now you're fawning all over the patients for all the world to see. I wonder what the BCA Disciplinary Committee would have to say about that?'

His grip on her shoulders was painfully tight as he towered over her like an avenging angel. His breathing was laboured, the warm rush of air brushing erratically over her face and stirring tendrils of coppery hair against her temples. His mouth was clamped shut into a tight, unforgiving line.

She gazed up at him half dazed by the speed with which events were happening, her heart slamming against her chest.

'What. . .what do you mean?' she stammered. 'What's going on?'

'That's what I want to know.' He gave her a stern glare. 'Who was that. . .the Romeo out there?'

Rebecca couldn't help it; his choice of words made her burst into helpless giggles—as much from a reaction to tension as anything else.

Alex stiffened with outrage.

'You think it's that funny to make a fool of me?' He was incensed, his eyes seeming to shoot sparks.

Rebecca's merriment died as she recognised the hurt hidden in his words and she felt her eyes brimming with tears. She would never want to hurt him. She loved him.

'What do you mean by flaunting your latest conquest under everyone's noses. Have you no sense of decency? No sense of shame?'

In his voice she could hear the same torment which filled her to overflowing.

'Well?' He shook her shoulders briefly when she didn't answer. 'What have you got to say for yourself? Becca. . .? Oh, God, Becca. I'm sorry. Please don't cry.'

A single solitary tear had made its way over her lashes and on to her cheek.

His hold on her shoulders softened into a caress and his hands slid around her to pull her tightly against him. One hand lifted to cradle her head as he gazed down into her face, his eyes darkening with emotion even as she watched.

'Becca,' he breathed softly. 'Oh, Becca. . .' and his hand tilted her face to receive his lips.

Gently, so very gently he sipped the solitary tear, the tip of his tongue coming out to lap at the silvery track it had left on her cheek. He lifted his head and his hands came up to frame her face.

'Oh, my love. . .' The words were whispered but they filled Rebecca's whole world and gave her the courage to raise her eyes until she gazed into his with all her emotions blazing. Her lips trembled as she saw his pupils darken and she answered brokenly.

'Alex. . . Oh, Alex, please. . .?'

For endless seconds he stared at her as if stunned and her heart sank within her, heavy with the weight of rejection.

A burning sensation behind her eyes warned her that a flood of misery and self-pity was not far away when suddenly, with a totally inarticulate groan, both his arms swept around her to enfold her convulsively against him.

For several long seconds he held her impossibly tightly until a shudder swept through him and he relaxed his hold just enough to allow her to breathe again.

Her face was pressed against his shoulder and she breathed in deeply his own individual musky smell overlaid by the clean tang of soap. With every fibre of her being she was aware of his powerful body.

For long heart-stopping moments they were still, almost without breathing, then Alex drew in a deep breath and loosened his hold enough to enable him to slide his hand round to cup her chin.

Deep inside she was conscious of a trembling which was growing and spreading until she was sure he must be able to feel it.

Slowly she raised her eyes so that they traversed the strong column of his throat to pause momentarily on the partly opened invitation of his lips before finally reaching the molten inferno of his eyes.

Their gazes locked and with a groan he caught her to him again in a fierce embrace and covered her mouth in a scorching kiss. Her response was like an explosion of white heat and he swung her up into his arms.

'Alex! No! You'll hurt your back!' she reminded him breathlessly.

'Not if you hold on,' he ordered, and she willingly complied as he carried her swiftly through the house, his eyes burning their message into hers.

She directed him towards her room, her euphoria at the thought of what was about to happen tempered by the quivering shyness creeping over her.

'*What the*——?' Alex had stopped dead at the door to her room, his whole body rigid. Disgust filled his expression as his eyes raked her abandoned pose in his arms and he released her abruptly.

'How many of us *are* there?' he ground out, his gaze once more fixed on something in the room.

Rebecca had almost fallen when her feet had hit the floor so suddenly, and it took her several seconds to turn and focus on the object of his anger—her rumpled, unmade bed.

'Why, you. . .' His implication scalded her and without a second thought she swung round, her palm striking his face with a sound like gunshot.

Before she had time to regret her descent into violence he moved, manacling each wrist in one of his hands and drawing them forcefully behind her back.

'You little vixen,' he hissed through gritted teeth. 'I should make you pay for that,' and he increased the pressure of her hands against the back of her waist.

'What did you expect me to do?' she flung up at him as he loomed over her. 'You insult me in such a vile way and I'm just expected to accept it?' She twisted against him trying to jerk her wrists out of his grasp, but his strength was supreme.

'The truth hurts, does it?' he sneered.

'Truth?' she scorned breathlessly. 'Alex, you wouldn't know what the truth was if it jumped up and bit you.' And she wrenched again at his confinement. 'Let me go,' she panted furiously, 'or is this the way you get your thrills?' She glared up at him, the dark brown of her eyes deepened by her anger, her chest rising and falling rapidly with the exertion.

'I've never taken a woman by force,' he bit out fiercely. 'I've never needed to!' and he lowered his head to take possession of her mouth.

The startled moment of stillness before she started to fight his domination was her downfall—it was all her body needed to recognise its unique counterpart.

With a groan of frustration that his grip on her hands prevented her from holding him she surged forward, her lips parting to invite his intimate trespass.

Alex tightened his grasp, pulling their bodies into total contact from their knees upwards. A brief adjustment transferred both her wrists to one powerful lean-fingered hand, leaving the other to spear through the thick coppery mass of her hair to cradle the back of her head.

'Becca,' he murmured thickly against her lips as he tilted her head to deepen the contact between their mouths.

'Mmm,' was her blissful reply as she invited his tongue to enter with teasing flicks of her own.

Suddenly realising that her hands were free, she lifted them to cradle each side of his face, stroking the slight rasp of regrowth over his jaw on her way to tracing the shape of his ears. He shuddered violently at the intimacy, one arm closing around her shoulders while the other dropped down to her hips, pulling her tightly against his taut thighs, against the evidence of his arousal.

Her hands slid upwards to tangle shaking fingers into

the crisp dark silk at the back of his head, encouraging and increasing the penetrating ardour of his kiss.

The slight hissing sound of a zip intruded briefly before he released her waistband and her skirt slithered downwards. Immediately his hand returned to stroke its way up under the crisp fabric of her hip-length white coat to find the edge of her blouse.

The searing contact of the warmth of his palm on the naked skin of her back was like a match to tinder. In seconds they were fighting furiously, this time to rid each other and themselves of the clothing which prevented them from seeing and touching each other.

Clumsy in their haste, fingers shaking uncontrollably as they tried to master ties and buttons, they were finally freed.

For endless seconds his eyes travelled over the creamy perfection of her body with the intensity of a caress.

'Dear God.' The words were torn huskily from his throat as he saw the matching longing in her eyes, and he swept her up to deposit her against the pillows.

The first contact of the full length of his naked body against her own made her gasp in wonder at the unexpectedly fiery heat and the slight roughness of the coating of dark silky body hair.

'You're so beautiful. So perfectly, utterly beautiful.' His voice was hoarse with emotion as his dark head swooped down to cover her mouth with a kiss of such fiercely controlled passion it left her lips trembling and swollen. His hand stroked up to encompass the soft weight of one pert, ripe breast.

'Alex!' She drew in a sharp breath of surprise at the unexpectedness of the sensation when he rolled her nipple between finger and thumb. The twist of desire coiled and tightened deep inside her, and she moved her legs in unknowing provocation, allowing his thigh to slide between hers, parting her legs and leaving her womanhood all too vulnerable to his questing hand.

The shock of the intimacy as he cupped her moist warmth with his palm held her rigid for several seconds until his mouth took possession of her lips again in a kiss of almost ferocious power.

He raised his head, his eyes piercing in their intensity.

'*This* is what it's all about.' His voice was impassioned as he tightened his grasp fractionally. 'This is the ultimate trust.' And his head came down to touch his lips to hers in a slow kiss.

In the space of those few seconds the fury was gone. Now, all was tenderness and perfect promise.

'Oh, Alex,' she whispered on a gasping breath as his mouth followed the contours of her breast, her ribcage and her waist.

'Touch me. . .please.' His voice was almost anguished in its huskiness as he took her hand in his and placed it on the dark silkiness of the hair on his leanly muscled chest.

She raised startled eyes to his before lowering them again to watch her fingers as she stroked them wonderingly through the whorls.

'Ahh.' He drew in a sharp breath as she raked her nails across him and caught one flat male nipple. With a cheeky grin, she repeated the manoeuvre, and with a shock felt a sharp movement against her thigh.

Her eyes found his again with a boldly questioning look. Alex took a deep shuddering breath and nodded slightly.

'If you want to.' The tone in his voice was an entreaty which became an impassioned moan as one slender hand trailed tantalisingly across the hard ridges of the muscles of his stomach until it finally met the aroused proof of his manhood.

He was still for a second, the molten steel of his gaze fixed fiercely on hers. Then, his head dropped back against the pillow in open surrender and her heart thudded violently in response to the small liquid sound of pleasure which emerged from his throat.

'Softly, sweetheart.' His voice was ragged. 'No more. Not yet.' His hands captured hers and carried them either side of her head on the pillow as the long lean length of his body covered hers.

He rested his weight on his forearms and watched her face knowingly as he lowered himself towards her, moving his torso from side to side so that he grazed the tips of her nipples. Her breasts tautened and swelled with instantaneous arousal and her eyes flew to his, the irises so widely dilated they appeared black.

'So responsive,' he murmured as one hand stroked over the creamy curve and moved on.

She was sensitive in places she had never realised, she thought as his strong fingers slid purposefully down her thigh to the back of her knee and then slipped to the exquisite sensitivity of her inner thigh.

Her momentary tension gave way to a trusting compliance so that when he silently urged it, she moved her leg, parting her thighs to accommodate his questing hand.

She froze.

'Relax, sweetheart,' he soothed, sliding the tip of his tongue around her parted lips in a caress which complemented perfectly the movement of his fingers.

Gradually his touch deepened, mimicking the sensuous movements of his tongue between her lips, until she moaned and moved sinuously under his hand.

'Yes.' His voice was a husky purr against her neck,

his warm sweet breath stirring the tendrils of hair against her ear. 'You like that, don't you?'

'Oh, Alex. . .please. . .' Desire had become a torrent of torment. 'I want. . .' her words were carried on breathless pants as her hips tilted upwards in the most graphic surrender of all.

'What, Becca? What do you want? This?' With one lithe movement he had positioned himself between her thighs so that the tumescent evidence of his own arousal was against her moist vulnerable core.

'Alex!' She closed her eyes and shuddered as he teased her, writhing against him so that they moved slickly together.

Finally he paused and murmured urgently. 'Sweetheart, open your eyes. Look at me.'

Her eyes, when she opened them, were dazed with desire, and he gave a shuddering groan as he visibly fought for control.

'Look at us. Look down at us.' And he directed her gaze towards the centre of all their sensations.

She gazed in wonder at the evidence of the extent of his desire for her. His fingers started moving again and she could see the tensing of the muscles and ligaments in his forearm at the same time as the touch of his fingertips started the sweet ache coiling again deep in the pit of her stomach.

'Watch us, sweetheart. Watch what happens.' Her eyes riveted to the point where their bodies met, she felt rather than saw the gentle pressure which finally joined the two of them with a shuddering surge of near ecstasy as they became one.

Alex paused briefly, watching the expression on her face as she felt her body relax to accommodate the intrusion.

'Now, sweetheart. Now,' he said as he started the

slow rhythm. 'I can't hold back any longer,' and he bent his head forward to take her mouth as completely as he was taking her body.

Rebecca felt a wildness rush through her. The threads of past events and present needs wove magic strands around them drawing them closer. . .closer. . .

The wildness grew as his mouth moved hungrily from one burgeoning breast to the other and she writhed against him, urging him to take all she had to give.

He thrust into her deeply and Rebecca found herself grasping his hips, trying to get closer to him when he made as if to withdraw.

'It's good. So good.' Her words were thready and breathless, but they were enough to snap his control and he arched repeatedly into her, filling her until she was consumed in the fire which swept them both.

'Becca. . .' The soft voice was accompanied by the gentle stroke of one fingertip as it ran over her eyebrow.

'Mmm?' She stretched lazily and turned over onto her back, unwilling to wake from the sensuous images which filled her mind.

'Becca. . .' the voice called again in her dream, and her dream lover—Alex—kissed her tenderly.

Only it wasn't a dream.

Her eyes snapped open, the besotted smile disappearing instantly she saw the dark outline looming over her.

'Alex. . .? What are you. . .?' She was having trouble focusing her thoughts. 'Oh. . .!' Remembrance flooded over her.

'You look so beautiful.' His voice was no more than a husky murmur as his eyes travelled over the body spread before him in sensuous abandon, their touch as potent as a caress.

'Oh, God!' Her hand flew out to grasp hold of the quilt, trying to pull it over herself as she realised that she was totally naked.

'It's a little late for that,' Alex chuckled as he put his hand over hers to still the frantic movement.

'Leave me alone!' she snapped, conscious of the flood of heat staining her cheeks, and rolled over to sit on the edge of the bed. 'Get out of my room.' She directed the words over her shoulder as she reached for the kimono she had left draped over the bedside chair.

There was an ominous silence behind her which was broken only by the sound of furious footsteps.

Unfortunately for her peace of mind they were not going in the direction of the door but led straight to the patch of carpet which had been the focus of her gaze.

Naked feet were planted squarely on her bedside rug, the darkly tanned skin contrasting vividly with the pale fluffy wool.

Her eyes travelled reluctantly up the tautly muscled shins and over his knees to the solid power of his thighs.

A sharp gasp and a flare of heat in her cheeks followed her discovery that he was totally and unashamedly naked.

Two lean hands reached into her field of vision to grip her by the shoulders and jerk her unceremoniously to her feet.

'If you like what you see so much, why are you trying to throw me out?' he demanded, his brows drawn down over glacial eyes.

'I wasn't. . . I didn't. . .' she flustered, trying to defend herself in spite of her increasing blushes.

'You were, and you did. . . We both did. . .and it was fantastic.' His eyes burned into hers, darkening visibly as he forced her to remember what had happened such a short time ago.

'That doesn't mean that you. . .that we. . .' She stumbled to a halt.

'Yes, it does,' he asserted forcefully. 'You didn't get to twenty-four years of age to waste your virginity on a one-night stand.' She gasped in mortification but he barely paused. 'And I certainly don't intend to be treated as a one-night stand, otherwise I'll know you don't respect me,' he finished piously.

Rebecca's eyes flew up to meet his in disbelief.

'But that's. . .'

'Stupid. Yes, I agree, but I've got my reputation to think of. What would people say if they knew what I'd let you do to my poor body. . .'

'Oh, Alex. Your back. . .!'

'Has never felt better and can't wait for another session of the same treatment.' He slid his hands from her shoulders and down her arms until he took one hand in each of his.

'Now, how about sitting down and telling me what this is really all about, hmm?'

She flicked a glance down over his chest and beyond and rapidly dragged her eyes back up.

'But you're not. . .'

'No, I'm not, am I. Well,' he conceded, 'just to spare my blushes when you can't help staring at me. . .' He turned away and fumbled among the tumbled pile of discarded clothes until he found his underpants. 'Better?' he queried as he stood up, 'Or do I have to go the whole way?'

Rebecca's eyes had been focused on the lean perfection of his tightly muscled buttocks when he turned towards her and he smiled knowingly.

'Enough of that,' he scolded gently, 'We've got a lot of talking to do before I can let you have your wicked way with me again.'

In spite of their humourous delivery, his words were sobering.

'Oh, Alex.' She shook her head. 'It's no good. We'll never be able to. . .'

'Never say never,' he admonished. 'You wait. It'll all come out right.'

'But how can it, when we can't agree on anything,' she wailed.

'Do you love me,' he demanded suddenly, his eyes fixed unwaveringly on hers.

'What. . .? Why. . .?' she halted, feeling horribly vulnerable being put on the spot like that.

'All right. I'll go first,' Alex continued. 'I love you, Rebecca James. Now, it's your turn.'

'I. . . You. . . Oh, Alex. . .!' And she burst into tears. 'Oh, Alex,' she cried against his chest as he gathered her close. 'Oh, I do love you. I didn't know you did and I wanted you to and I've loved you for such a long time, but it's no good,' she sobbed.

'It sounds pretty good to me,' he comforted as he reached for a handful of tissues to start mopping up.

'But you don't trust me,' she accused sadly. 'You can't accept my profession, and I can't just g-give it up. . .' the tears started to fall again.

'I do trust you,' he said quietly. 'In fact, I'm willing to trust you with my life. I'm putting all my happiness for the rest of my life in your hands.' The seriousness of his tone had silenced her tears instantly.

'But how can you say that?' she accused. 'You haven't even trusted me enough to tell me why you hate chiropractic!' she raked the fingers of both hands through the tear-dampened tangled copper of her hair.

'It's not chiropractic,' he said wearily, 'or at least only in as much as it's an alternative or complementary therapy. And even then it's probably guilt as much as anything else.'

'Guilt? Why should you feel guilty?'

'Because of my sister.' The words were almost inaudible.

'You mentioned her once before, didn't you? What happened? What did you do that makes you feel guilty?'

'Nothing.' The one word was heavy with regrets.

'But. . . I don't understand.'

'I'm sorry.' He shook his head. 'It won't make sense unless I tell you the whole story, but. . .' He raised his shoulders in a shrug.

'Why don't you start by telling me about her?' Rebecca suggested gently. 'Is she older or younger?'

'Younger, by five years—or at least she was.' His voice was pensive as he remembered.

'Was?' Rebecca's tone was shocked.

'She's dead,' his voice had that hollow tone she had heard several times before. 'And it was such a waste. . .such a criminal waste of a life. . .'

Rebecca put her arms around him in an automatic gesture of comfort, her head coming to rest in the curve of his shoulder.

'She was a singer.' His breath teased her hair as he spoke over her head. 'Opera, not pop, although she loved singing anything. . .' He paused, but Rebecca knew he would continue in his own time.

'She had a bit of trouble with her throat and I put her in contact with one of the top specialists—it can help being in the trade!' His own arm had encircled her and he gave her a squeeze.

'Apparently, the problem was being caused by a small lesion on her vocal cords.'

'Oh, no!' Alex glanced down at her and smiled bleakly.

'By all accounts it should have responded well to radiation. The prognosis was good as far as her singing was concerned. She was told it should have little or no effect on her vocal cords.'

He shook his head. 'I was so busy with my own career at that point that I more or less wrote the whole situation off as satisfactorily completed. Even when she came to me for money, I didn't think to ask what it was for. I just presumed it was to pay the bills for the specialist.'

He was silent for so long that she knew the next part of the story was crucial

'It was nearly four months before I found out what she had done.' His voice was a terrible mixture of anger and grief. 'She was talking to some man at a party, and somehow he persuaded her that she was risking her voice with the radiotherapy, and that he knew a far better way.

'Four months!' His hand clenched unconsciously on her shoulder. 'Four months of taking coloured water that she paid the earth for, and "prescribed" by someone who had no qualifications of any sort. Just a con artist after her money—my money.' His disgust was total.

'In the end, when her throat felt no better, she went back to the specialist.'

The silence throbbed. Rebecca drew back just enough to look up at his face. His eyes were grey desolation.

'She was told that the tumour had progressed in those four months. It was no longer suitable for radiotherapy. He told her that surgery was the only option, and that he couldn't even guarantee if she'd be able to speak afterwards, let alone sing.'

'What happened?' Rebecca questioned softly. 'Was the surgery unsuccessful?'

'She never went for surgery.' He closed his eyes tight, the thick dark lashes forming shadowy crescents on his cheekbones as he shook his head. 'When she realised she'd never sing opera again, she committed suicide.'

'Oh, Alex, no!'

'I went after the bastard, as soon as I found out what had been going on, but he was long gone. Apparently he had several people hooked; all wealthy, except for Laura. She was the only one buying the coloured water as a cancer cure. The others believed it would keep them young and beautiful. Evidently, he swotted up on just enough technical terms to pull the wool over their eyes. . .' He took a deep breath and released it slowly.

'I should have been there for her. I should have found out what was going on. I could have investigated that rat and shown her what he was in time to. . .' His throat had closed, preventing speech.

'But, Alex, it wasn't your fault.' She put her hand over his mouth when he went to argue. 'If she was anything like you, she would have been one very determined lady.' She paused and raised one eyebrow.

He nodded, his eyes eloquent.

'In which case I don't suppose anyone could have stopped her, once she had decided what she wanted to do.'

His hand came up to cover hers, and he planted a

kiss in her palm before curling her fingers over to contain it.

'You're quite right, you know. I just hadn't thought of it like that before.' He huffed out an exasperated breath. 'She had ample opportunity to speak to me when she asked me for money to pay the swine, but she kept it to herself.'

Their eyes met and held in a long communion before Rebecca finally braved the final question.

'So, when your mother wanted to come to me, you transferred all your guilt and anger over Laura's death on to me?'

'I know it's not logical. . .'

'But then, when has anger ever been logical?'

'Oh, Becca, what did I ever do to deserve you? How did you put up with all that aggression?'

'I don't know. It must be my placid saintly nature, I suppose,' she answered, straight-faced.

Alex lifted his head slowly to gaze at her, then hooted.

'You? Placid? Saintly? You were a sharp-tongued fire-breathing witch! Talk about fighting your corner! I hardly got a word in while you harangued me the way you wanted to rant at your father.'

'Yes, well,' she felt the warmth in her cheeks, 'I suppose it's my turn to apologise for punishing you for someone else's sins.'

'But, Becca, I am glad you and your parents are getting along better. If anything happened to them, you would have felt terrible knowing there had been a rift between you.'

'You're really serious about this "families stick together" business, aren't you?' she smiled up at him.

'You can never have too much family,' he said, with so much feeling that Rebecca was amazed.

'If you're so serious about it, why haven't you married and had your own family?'

'Is that a fishing expedition?' he teased. 'If so, I hope you're pleased that you've caught something. Now, it just remains to find out if you're going to throw it back.'

'Throw what back?' Rebecca's heartbeat was racing. He couldn't really mean what she thought, could he?'

'Me.' He leant forward until their foreheads met and stroked the tip of her nose with his own. 'You've got me well and truly hooked, so please be merciful and put me out of my misery quickly.'

He slanted his head and took her lips in a tender kiss.

'Alex!' She was breathless when he lifted his head.

'Is that a yes?' he demanded.

'To what?'

'You're going to make me say it, aren't you?' He smiled.

'Say what?' she teased, her spirits so high she felt as if she was floating.

'That I love you.' His tone was mock-exasperated.

'Only if you mean it.' She met his eyes fearlessly.

'Oh, yes, Becca, I mean it.' His arms tightened around her as he devastated her with his kiss.

'Oh, Alex, I love you, too,' she breathed.

'We'll get married as soon as we can get our parents together,' he pronounced. 'It shouldn't take more than a week to organise and then we can——'

'Hey!' she interrupted with her hand over his mouth again.

'What?' he mumbled through her fingers, taking advantage of the position to touch her palm sensuously with the tip of his tongue.

'What wedding?' she demanded. 'No one's proposed to me yet. Ahh. . .!'

With a sudden flurry of limbs Alex had toppled her over on to her back on the bed and followed her down to pin her arms over her head.

She tried to wriggle out from under him, but he quickly restrained her with one powerful thigh.

'Alex!' she squealed as one hand lingered over her vulnerable ribs. 'Don't tickle me, please. Please!'

She was captivated by the mischievous gleam in his eyes as his fingers hovered over her.

'What's it worth, not to tickle you?' he bargained.

'A k-kiss?' she giggled.

'How about an answer?'

'To what?' she tried to sound innocent. 'No. . . no! Don't! I give in! All you have to do is ask me nicely.'

'How nicely?' he growled. 'This nicely?' and his head came down over hers, pausing at the barest shadow of contact to stroke her lips softly with his.

The tension was there between them, exactly as it had been from the first time they had met, and she flicked the tip of her tongue out to moisten her lips.

The simultaneous contact with his lips drew a deep groan from his chest, and the echoes vibrated against her breasts, eliciting an answering moan of surrender from her.

His control disappeared and he ravaged her mouth, his ardour parting her lips to meet the tongue enticing him to explore the sweetness within.

Time had no meaning for them until they collapsed, breathless, beside each other.

'Was that nicely enough?' he demanded hoarsely when he had recovered enough to speak.

'I'm thinking. . .' she said pensively.

'About whether you want to marry me?' There was a tinge of outrage in his voice.

'No, about whether you asked me nicely enough. Perhaps you ought to have another try. . . No! Alex! Don't!'

'Well, then. What's your answer?' He had rolled over suddenly, belying his apparent exhaustion, and had her at his mercy again.

'Yes, Alex. Please.' She managed to lift her head just enough to touch his lips in a fleeting kiss. 'I love you and I'll marry you as soon as you like.'

'Oh, Becca.' Could that be relief she heard in his voice? 'I love you too.'

'In spite of the alternative. . .?' She didn't get a chance to finish her question before he interrupted.

'Alternative nothing,' Alex silenced her with a fierce kiss. 'There is no alternative for you, Becca. You're my one and only.'

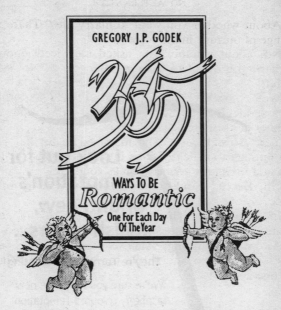
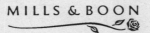

Look out for Temptation's bright, new, stylish covers...

They're Terrifically Tempting!

We're sure you'll love the new raspberry-coloured Temptation books—our brand new look from December.

Temptation romances are still as passionate and fun-loving as ever and they're on sale now!

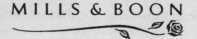

MILLS & BOON